COLOURS OF DEATH 2

SERGEANT THOMAS: FURTHER CASEFILES

ROBERT NEW

National Library of Australia Cataloguing-in-Publication entry:
Creator: New, Robert, author.
Title: Colours Of Death 2: Sergeant Thomas: Further Casefiles
ISBN: 9780648681687
Subjects: Detective fiction short stories.

Tale Publishing
Melbourne Victoria

Other Books by
Robert New

Sergeant Thomas

Colours of Death: Sergeant Thomas' Casebook
Incite Insight (A Novel)

Novels

Sovereign Assassin
The Conversationist

Short Story Collections

Mug Punter: Three Capers
Movemind: Speculative Short Stories

For Children

Eddy's Treasure (written with Michael New)
Unicorn's Egyptian Rescue (written with Rachel New)

Contents

Red
Poison Fire

When dispatch called Sergeant Brad Thomas, he couldn't imagine how odd this new case would become, especially since it appeared so straightforward. A cleaner had gone to a large house in Wembley for her usual duties. When she let herself in, she discovered the lady of the house collapsed on the floor. A touch of the neck looking for a pulse revealed the body was cold. Paramedics confirmed the death and asked detectives to attend the scene as there were signs of foul play. Brad usually found such cases relatively easy to solve. It was almost always the husband in a case like that.

Brad assigned the investigation to Detective Sally Summers and himself. They drove the ten minutes to the scene without having to battle much mid-morning traffic on the hot summer day.

As they drove around Lake Monger to the house, Brad began to look forward to his next run around the three-and-a-half kilometre track which bordered the lake. It was a weekly ritual, which he shared on alternate weekends with his wife, Amy, or the city's senior medical examiner, Samantha.

The house was modern, and located near to the top of a hill overlooking the western side of the lake and parkland. Brad had admired the façade of the house numerous times on his jogs. He never thought he would get to go inside, let alone have to investigate a potential murder within it.

Brad felt his calves stretch as he walked up the steep driveway to the house. He was reminded he'd skipped last week's run due to his wife spending the morning throwing up. At the front door, he was greeted by a paramedic he recognised from the disaster at the Sangre Azul school a few years before. She had a face mask dangling from one ear. Both their heads twitched in recognition as Brad approached. He tried desperately to remember her name, but try as he might, it wouldn't come to him. He decided to start with an approach which would give her an opportunity to introduce herself.

"Hi. I'm Brad, we met when there was the mass poisoning at Blue Bloods. This is Sally. She's my co-lead on this case."

Sally reached out to shake hands.

"Hi, Sally, I'm Emma." That was it. *Emma.* "I'm sorry we couldn't meet under more pleasant circumstances." Emma's last sentence held a slightly rote cadence, but Brad couldn't help but admire the expression. It was a good way of introducing yourself to people who were experiencing trauma, which was pretty much what Emma had to do on a daily basis.

"What've we got?" Brad asked.

"Luke and I arrived half an hour ago. We found the woman, Desola Rhamnousia, face down on the kitchen floor. Her phone was on the floor a metre away."

Emma pulled her mask back over her mouth. Brad and Sally each put on one of their own. Emma led them through the house. Brad admired the large white tiles covering the floor. He decided they must have had a drop or two of red dye in them as they appeared 'warmer' than other white tiles he'd seen. It avoided the sterile look some modern homes had. Maybe that would be a good surface for the second bedroom Brad and his wife were going to redecorate?

"The phone screen is cracked, so it seems like she was trying to make a call for help when she collapsed and dropped it. We got the shock of our lives when we turned the body over to examine for signs of life." Emma stopped in a doorway and faced the detectives. "I thought I'd seen everything. Turns out there was at least one more thing for me to see."

Emma stepped aside. Brad tried not to gag as he entered the room. The body wasn't decomposed, nor full of maggots, like he'd started picturing. Nor was it the scent. It was the face which stood out; it was peeling off.

"My god," Brad said involuntarily.

Sally, like Brad, took a couple of paces backward and turned slightly to the side, but still kept glancing at the body. "Has her face melted? What *is* that?" she asked.

"Best we can tell is that the skin on her face is so

degraded it's falling off. I'm not a medical examiner, but I don't think it was something done to her, if you know what I mean. Like, no one's peeled it or anything," Emma said.

Luke, the second paramedic, handed Brad a piece of paper. "The cleaner left her contact details for you. She couldn't bring herself to stay here with the body."

"Sorry, guys, you'll need to see this," Emma said, calling them closer to the body. She pointed to the facial expression on the corpse. Desola's face, or what could be seen of it, was clearly contorted into what looked like a grimace of pain.

"That's horrible. How long must she have suffered to get like this? Why didn't she ask anybody to help her?" Brad asked.

"Maybe someone prevented her?" Sally said.

"I imagine you'll have to work that out," Emma said good-naturedly. The cue was enough for Brad to overcome his repulsion of the scene and switch to detective mode. It seemed to do the same for Sally, as they both put on gloves. The photographing, bagging and tagging around the body took a few minutes. Sally turned to Brad.

"Are we looking for anything in particular?"

"How about potential poisons? The death seems grotesque and unnatural. There must be something which will give us a clue as to what transpired to bring about Desola's death."

Brad liked to use victim's names when investigating a crime. It made the case seem more personal and he used it as additional motivation to solve the mystery. He didn't want to become one of those cops who seemed to forget a victim was someone's child or loved one. He didn't want murder investigations to be reduced to statistics. Whatever he saw, however badly he knew people could treat each other, he had to still believe humanity was inherently good and by catching the few bad apples he was making the world a better place for now and the next generation.

"She hasn't been dead all that long, as her temperature's still around thirty degrees – cold to the touch but not all that cold. Like I said, this isn't natural decomposition. I don't think we're at risk of catching anything. If it was something in the air it would've affected the cleaner, but she was fine. Keep your masks and gloves on all the same," Emma said.

"Thanks, Emma, we've finished with the body. Can you take it to the city morgue? I know Samantha will want to get in on this one."

"Sure." The paramedics loaded the body onto a stretcher and into the ambulance. Brad walked to the door to see them out and catch a breath of fresh air. From the doorway he looked at the houses nearby. How many, if any, of the neighbours spying on the property would understand the implications of no sirens or lights being used as the ambulance departed?

Brad and Sally began a thorough search of the house. Brad couldn't get the image of Desola's contorted grotesque face out of his mind. It was a myth perpetuated by schlocky crime novels that the body kept its final facial expression after death. But if muscles had seized due to a toxin, and the body lay with the face held in that position, then it was feasible for the expression to be retained. Regardless, Desola's face would haunt him. Her skin was like the scene in the Indiana Jones movie when the Nazi's opened the arc and their faces started melting.

Brad's search found only the usual household chemicals in the downstairs floor of the house. The kitchen was spotlessly clean, and the contents of the fridge were all well organised. Brad checked dates on the jars in case there was some form of food poisoning involved, but everything was in-date and had no signs of any mould or bacterial growth. Nevertheless, he bagged a few items for testing, then made his way upstairs.

He found Sally in the master bedroom, which overlooked the parkland and lake to the east.

"That bed tells a story," Brad said.

"What story is that?" Sally replied.

"Well, look at the indentations. It's clearly a mattress they've had for a while. New ones don't hold the shape like that. The indents are so far apart. That is not a happy marriage; they sleep as far away as possible from each other. My bed isn't like that. Amy and I are literally rolled into each other when we go to sleep. Our indentation is in the middle."

"But you've only been married for a couple of years."

"So?"

"So, you're still *honeymooners*. Wait 'til you've been married for decades and see how you sleep. Better yet, wait till you've had kids. My parents' bed has always looked like that and they've been married for forty-five years. You're overthinking things. For once, turn off that part of your brain and just accept that some people like their own space."

Brad raised his eyebrows and smiled. "You have a point. But still, maybe we should look at the husband?"

Sally nodded. "Where is he anyway?"

"Business trip. He gets back tomorrow evening."

"How can you possibly know that?"

"There was a whiteboard on the fridge. It had their schedules for the week. Desola was due at a bowls club meeting tomorrow at one. The club's just over there."

Without looking, Brad pointed out the window towards the lake. The bowls club was between the lake and the house. "I run past it all the time," Brad explained.

He moved to the bathroom, where there was a double-basined bench, large shower, bath and toilet. Desola and her husband clearly had a sink to themselves, for each space on the bench had its own set of toiletries. Brad found some sputum on the rim of the toilet towards the front, and some fecal matter towards the back. He carefully scraped them into specimen jars.

"I'll get started outside," Sally said. Brad nodded and she left to search the backyard.

Half an hour later, Sally and Brad conferred before leaving the property.

"There was a greenhouse out back. Lots of pots of veggies and fruit trees. A few flowers, some goodlooking chillies too. I was so tempted to take some. Something about it though. I can't say why, but the layout and organisation seemed somehow masculine. Does that make sense?"

Brad laughed. "Not really. But we'll go with it being the hubby's hobby then."

~

A short drive took them back to the station. They'd arranged for the cleaner to meet them there, 'to assist with their enquiries'. The cleaner was a young Aboriginal woman, Aja. Brad was struck by how she held herself. She seemed to embody someone who was comfortable in their skin and driven to succeed. She was intelligent too. Her response to Brad confirming she was the Rhamnousia's cleaner, was that where else could a twenty-year-old with no experience earn thirty dollars an hour while putting themselves through uni? She could set her own hours, work at odd times and not have to deal with workplace politics. A good audiobook or playlist made the work a breeze. If only he'd been as switched on at her age.

"So, what did you see when you approached the house and discovered Ms Rhamnousia?" Brad asked.

The smaller of the stations' two interview rooms wasn't brightly lit and was designed to be cosy. The atmosphere was usually one of a confessional, but today Aja's presence made it seem like a sanctuary. Brad and Sally exchanged looks. Sally's expression showed him that Aja had affected her in the same way.

"The house was as it always was. The gardener keeps the front immaculate and mows that tiny strip of lawn out the back, but I think you probably saw how that area is dominated by the greenhouse. It's Andre's refuge. I only met him a few times, and that's where he always went after a brief hello. I'm not sure how much he liked his wife."

"Go on," Sally prompted.

"I let myself in, as I usually do. I wasn't expecting anyone to be home. Desola usually comes back from the bowls club in time to pay me. She's the club secretary. She spends a lot of time there, though that might be due to the cheap drinks from the bar."

Sally jotted that on the pad in front of her.

"I don't think she had a lot of friends. The bowls club was her main social outlet and despite everyone knowing her, she didn't think she really belonged. Most were just too old for her to relate to."

"You say 'she didn't think'; she spoke to you about her loneliness?" Brad queried.

"Yes. Sometimes we'd share a coffee before I left and talk about things. I'm a good listener, and she'd often tip me after a good chat. I think that's how she related to people. If she found our chat valuable to her then she thought it was worth paying for. It made me feel weird though, as it seemed so … transactional."

Brad found himself admiring the young woman once again. Her vocabulary and awareness were exemplary. He hoped a child of his would be like that when they were an adult.

"A couple of months ago, just after she'd been to Queensland with her husband, she told me she thought he was having or wanted to have an affair with his secretary. It was a cliché she couldn't bear."

Sally's pen flew across the page once more.

"She wouldn't give Andre the satisfaction of a divorce, especially since he gave her so much grief over being barren."

"She couldn't have kids?" Sally asked.

"No. It caused a rift between them. I think he compensated with his greenhouse. At least he could grow and nurture things to maturity."

The insight was remarkable. "Sorry for interrupting your narrative, but I have to know. What are you studying at uni?"

"Arts. I'm doing a major in psych. I'm intending to do a Master of Teaching and get my psych registration afterwards so I can be a school counsellor."

"That's impressive," Brad said.

"Thanks. Desola also didn't want to divorce him because, as she told me, she still loved him despite her anger at how he treated her."

"When did she say that?" Sally asked.

"Just after the Queensland trip. Her mood seemed to pick up a bit after that. Though my impressions are mostly based on short interactions, so maybe I'm imagining it. It was the week after the long weekend."

"Okay. Thanks. Where in Queensland did they go? Surfers? Noosa?"

"Cairns, but nearer the forest. Redlynch Valley? Maybe. Something like that. They did a web booking for a house.

Desola was delighted when they got it."

"What happened after you let yourself in?" Brad asked.

"I went to the kitchen. It's where I usually dump my things while I clean. That's when I discovered her. She was lying on her front. When I touched her neck it was cold. I couldn't feel a pulse. I took out my phone and called the emergency line. Then I took my stuff and went out the front and sat on the step."

Aja's composure began to falter. "I c-couldn't be in there with her like that. I could tell she was dead."

"Did you touch anything inside the house?"

"No. I mean I dropped my bag when I saw her and picked it up as I went out the front, but otherwise, no, I don't think so. How long had she been like that? The poor lady."

A tear welled in Aja's eye. Her empathy was infectious, and Brad found himself feeling concern over how Desola's body had lain there, how terrible it must have been to die alone.

"Did you see anything?" Sally asked.

"No. The house felt empty when I arrived. I mean, like no one was home. That's normal. It's why I listen to something while I clean. It helps me stop paying attention to the fact I'm disturbing the silence."

"Sorry for what I'm about to ask. Did Andre ever try anything romantic with you?" Sally asked.

Aja looked surprised. "No. I'm too young for him. As I said, I think he was interested in his secretary. Desola said something about her having reached the age where her biological clock was ticking; that was a sirens' call for Andre."

"Anything else we should know?"

Aja shook her head. "I can't think of anything."

Brad gave her his card and asked Aja to call if she thought of something to add. Sally helped Aja find her way out, while Brad sat in silence. A minute later Sally breezed back into the room.

"It's got to be the husband," Sally said.

"It almost always is. But let's wait for the ME's report to confirm murder before we go meeting planes and making dramatic airport arrests.

Sally smiled. "I haven't done one of those before. Could be fun."

~

When Samantha, the medical examiner, called that evening, Brad was tidying his desk in preparation to leave for the day. He was keen to get home to his wife, Amy, who'd been unwell that morning.

"That body was extraordinary. Honestly, there's no other word for it," Samantha began. Her delight at the unusual manner of death was something Brad had experienced before.

"How so?"

"There were signs she'd been vomiting and had diarrhoea."

"That's what I thought from the samples I sent, so what's got you so excited?"

"It had been happening for more than a day, which

means she may have had a fever. That could mean we need to revise the time of death to earlier than we thought."

"The husband left three days ago. Could she have died around then?"

"That's probably too far. Maybe yesterday rather than this morning."

"Good to know."

"It was her internals which threw me. She had multiple organ failure, including acute kidney failure and liver necrosis. There's no way she wasn't in extreme pain, nor unaware she needed medical intervention."

"So, we're back to the question of why she didn't seek help. I asked Sally the same thing. I mean, with a house like that, money wasn't a problem, and emergency departments are free. She could afford an ambulance even if she didn't have that covered on her insurance."

Samantha's tone softened. "The only thing I can think is that she was confused. She almost certainly would've had problems with voluntary movement and experienced a speech impediment…"

"Your deliberate trailing off means you want me to ask the obvious question."

"Well, go on then."

"Fine. How could you know that?"

"Because her brain had shrunk!"

"Huh? Was she pregnant? Doesn't that happen during pregnancy?"

"Reading up on that are we? Any reason why?"

Brad inhaled sharply.

"Ooh," Samantha said. Fortunately, she let the moment pass. "No. She wasn't pregnant, though at forty-three, that wasn't quite out of the question, and for the record the woman's brain regains its size afterward. I don't know what could have caused it in Desola. Usually, I'd suspect Alzheimer's, but she was young. Not to mention, when I sectioned her brain and looked at it under a microscope, there weren't the plaques or tangles I'd have expected to see if that was the case."

"So, what could've made it happen?"

"That's what's bugging me. I can't think of a single thing which explains it all. I could give you many reasons for each symptom; necrosis of the liver could mean she's an alcoholic or overdosed on paracetamol, renal failure could be from untreated diabetes. You can lose ninety percent of your kidney function before you'd notice, so it could have been a chronic condition. The renal failure probably explains the vomiting and diarrhoea. But none of those fully explain the shrunken brain."

"So…"

"I'll have to do some research, but there's no way she died from natural causes."

"Understood. We'd pretty much figured that out though. The cleaner said Desola was perfectly healthy when she saw her last week."

"See, that's weird. Her internals were stuffed up. But at least that makes a poison of some sort the most likely modus operandi."

Brad decided to let the slight misuse of the term slide.

"Right. Maybe we can go back to the house tomorrow and search together? You might know what to look for more than me."

"You did well with what you bagged and tagged, but what we're dealing with here isn't run of the mill. How about I see you there at 8.30 am and we walk a lap of the lake before going in? I'll call into the office on the way and try to have some tox screen results with me," Samantha said.

"I might need a walk after rather than before. I'll need to clear my head after going back in there. It'll trigger flashbacks to that face."

"It made me react and I go through a body's internals most days. So, I agree it was hideous. See you at the usual place at 8.30 am then."

~

The sun shone brightly and the cool morning air was already showing signs of warming up when Brad and Samantha arrived at the lake. Samantha was wearing her usual work clothes – black pants and white shirt – and her hair was in a ponytail.

"Still up for that walk after?" Samantha asked.

"Yep."

They followed the path round from the car park to the bowls club, then across the expanse of grass to the road. The house was on the other side of the road, a few houses up from the path.

Brad let them in using the key Aja had given him. The house was as Brad remembered it: grand without being ostentatious. The high ceilings and white paint gave the place a light, airy feel Brad hadn't noticed the day before. He hoped there would be some clue he'd similarly missed.

After two hours of meticulous searching, they met back in the kitchen. Neither had found anything of note, though each had taken a few extra samples for testing. "Are we done in the house?" Samantha asked.

"I guess so. Just the greenhouse to go."

Once inside the greenhouse, Brad was struck by the space. It was the size of a double garage. There was a horseshoe of benches opening towards the door, and then two central benches in the middle. The back bench was a series of hydroponic set ups, growing mostly herbs and tomatoes, while the rest of the bench space was filled with potted plants. Brad was surprised nothing other than bags of potting mix and hydroponic supplies were on the floor. All the plants were at working height on the benches. Each plant had its own hydration monitor. Samantha pointed to a test kit for working out the nutrient content of the soil. "No wonder each plant looks so stunningly healthy," she said. "Andre is clearly obsessed."

Samantha took a rose by the stem and held it to her nose. "You've got to smell this, if not for the scent, then because you should stop and smell the roses."

Brad dutifully gave the rose a sniff. "That is good. Do you see anything here which could have caused Desola's symptoms?"

Samantha wandered slowly round the room. She occasionally touched some of the plants. "This chilli doesn't feel right, plus it seems to be all fruit and not tree."

She pointed to a bright red mass in a pot of soil. It had five 'fingers' and looked a little like the hand of a baby devil sticking out of the ground. It seemed out of place as it made the number of plants uneven between benches. It still had a soil monitor though.

"Take a sample then," Brad suggested.

Samantha used scissors to cut the top off one of the fingers of the fire-like mass.

"Dammit," she said with annoyance. "I've got a hole in my glove. Must've been the rose."

"Not to worry. It's not like there's anything here that needs a DNA sample."

"Yeah, I know you're right. It just startled me that's all. I didn't feel it happen."

Brad grinned. "Well, you were stopping to smell the roses."

"When I should have been saying 'by the pricking of my thumbs, something wicked this way comes'," Samantha cackled.

"We don't know how wicked yet."

"I'll run some tests on this and the rest of the samples and let you know when I've got something to report. We might have to skip that walk. This took longer than I thought."

"That's okay. I have to meet Sally at the airport. We're going to meet the husband as he gets off a plane."

"You have a photo?"

"Yes, from his driver's licence and the framed photos

on their living room wall. Though it seems those were from happier times. He'll have aged a bit, but at least we'll know what he looks like."

~

By the time Brad and Sally had met at the airport, and arranged to meet the plane, Brad had received a message from Samantha to say the sample she had taken was of a fungus, which meant it could easily have caused death since several species were poisonous. They went to a coffee stand and each bought a coffee to sip while they waited.

"You know, this is quite the nice change of pace. I mean, we know exactly where the suspect will be and at what time. They can't alter their fate unless they jump out of the plane, so we don't have to stress over getting somewhere as fast as possible."

"It's good, isn't it? Meeting a plane to speak to a suspect will be a first for me."

"Me too."

They were grateful Andre was coming from Sydney. As a domestic flight, getting to the gate was simple, though they still had to have to have a federal police officer with them. Thankfully, the policeman said he was content to hang back while Brad and Sally approached Andre to ask him to help with their enquiries.

"Remember, he probably doesn't know Desola is dead," Brad cautioned.

"Or will he?"

"I guess that is the question," Brad replied.

"Ooh, is that our plane?" Sally pointed to one taxiing

towards the gate.

"Looks like it." A nod from the federal police officer confirmed it was the one.

The plane docked and a few minutes later the first passengers started walking from the gangway to the lounge.

Both Brad and Sally kept glancing from a photo in Brad's hand to the passengers.

Sally gestured to someone. "That's him."

Brad tucked the photo into his pocket, as he, Sally and the federal officer approached.

Andre was tall, well-built and had just a few flecks of grey in his neatly combed brown hair. A line of stubble indicated he hadn't shaved that morning, but was that due to nerves about coming home or just laziness?

Andre turned to look behind him as the three of them approached. That wasn't the action of a guilty person. He was looking to see who they were after. His surprise that they wanted him was evident.

"Excuse me, Andre, we need you to come with us please," Brad said.

"Why? What have I done?"

"Please come with us. We'll talk in the airport's security room."

Brad couldn't read what Andre was thinking. He seemed surprised but not particularly concerned by being taken aside.

Once in the meeting room, the federal officer said, "Mr Rhamnousia, we've asked you here bec—"

"I know, routine search. I'm overdue for such an experience. I wasn't expecting it to be a strip search though."

Brad startled, then studied Andre's face. "No, I'm sorry to inform you that you wife has died."

"Oh, thank god," Andre said.

Sally's expression was startled. "I'm sorry?"

"Oh, shit, yeah, that might sound bad. I'm just relieved I don't have to strip. Look, I know you're doing your job, but I'm not about to mourn her. We weren't exactly getting along. Look, I probably should've said that's terrible and my life as I know it is over, but here's the thing: her dying would be such a relief. I don't mind confessing I wanted her out of my life, but she wouldn't grant me a divorce without a fight, nor leave the house, and in these stuffed up economic times, I can't afford a drawn out dispute. That's why I was in Sydney; my firm is working out how we can best inform clients their money has gone backwards."

Brad raised his eyebrows.

"I'm an investment banker. While the share market has gone up recently, our investments have been more long-term oriented. The short-term risk of negative returns has, unfortunately, eventuated, but we're confident there will be a recovery and the client's funds will not only be restored next year, but experience growth as well."

"Is that what you're telling them?" Sally asked.

"Almost word for word. We'll see if it works."

"And that takes five days to work out? Your schedule

was on the fridge," Brad said. "You also didn't answer our calls."

"If I'm being honest, I also needed some time away. Desola hasn't been easy to live with. As I said, I'd asked her for a divorce, but she would neither grant it, nor leave. So, yeah, I extended the trip a bit and stopped answering calls. How did she die? Let me guess. Car accident? She always felt driving was a sport rather than a means of transportation."

Andre's callousness over his wife's death was a change from the norm. Brad couldn't decide if it was incriminating or exonerating. He still hadn't seemed to grasp they were thinking about murder, and he was their suspect.

"We think it was poisoning," Brad said.

"Oh. *Oh.* So this isn't a chat to let me know, it's an interrogation. You think I had something to do with it. I guess I should've watched what I said. Do I need a lawyer?"

"At the moment you're just helping us with our enquiries," Brad replied calmly.

"I don't know what you've uncovered or who you've spoken to, but I'll guess you've heard about how I acted stupidly when we had trouble conceiving. I've apologised for how I behaved. But she wouldn't even let me consider adopting. I want to be a father. She wouldn't even let me have a puppy."

"But?"

"But I didn't kill her. I couldn't. I'm about nurturing life, not destroying it. Did you see my greenhouse?"

"We'd like to take your computer for analysis, if you're willing to give it voluntarily?" Brad asked.

"Take it. Though any financial records relating to my work are confidential. The password is parous!#1h."

Andre took his laptop from his bag and slid it over the small table to Brad. "You said poison. Any particular one? Or did she just down a bottle of vodka?"

"We're not totally sure yet. Her body was found two days ago, and the medical examiner is still running pathology on samples from the autopsy," Brad said.

"How did you get consent for an autopsy?"

"When the death is suspicious, we don't need permission from the next of kin."

"Oh. I didn't know that."

Andre showed mild surprise but didn't seem ruffled. Brad couldn't read if Andre was a very cool killer, a very unloving husband, or both.

"Can I see her?" Andre asked.

"I'll arrange a viewing with the medical examiner. Would tomorrow morning suit?"

"I guess so."

Brad took Andre's contact details and said he'd return the computer the next day.

~

Sally nudged Brad on the way out. "You know, despite the fact he might be a killer, it was refreshing to hear a man talk about wanting to be a dad."

Brad's head twitched. "Why wouldn't a man want to be a dad? Is that a rare quality?"

"In my dating experience, yes."

"Shame. You'd be a great mum."

"When are you and Amy going to, you know?"

"When we're ready."

"Hmmm." Sally eyed him as though she didn't trust the answer. "You've been extra smiley recently."

"When we're ready," Brad repeated. He didn't want to say he and Amy had been trying for eight months now.

"I'm going to take this to forensics. How about you work on one of your other cases for a bit?

"Sure, there's a run of the mill car crash which needs looking over."

~

Brad was about to finish his shift when an email from James, the forensic IT specialist of the team, stopped him in his tracks. James, like Brad, must've been putting in some overtime, since it was already 6.00 pm. It was the preliminary report on Andre's computer.

Hi Brad,

I've done a cursory analysis of the computer for you. There are a lot of password protected files, but these do seem to be client related for the investment banking which you said the owner does. I'll do a more in-depth analysis in the morning and look at erased files. There's only one odd thing so far. There's a bookmark for a page, but no browsing history to it, despite there being a full browsing history for the last year. That's the sort of thing which happens when you accidentally bookmark something during private browsing. They must've thought it wouldn't save. The page was for bit.ly/3g3tUz7. I'll give you an update by 10 am tomorrow.

-James

Brad clicked on the link. It opened to a newspaper article about a type of fungi called a poison fire coral. The article outlined that consumption of it would lead to all the symptoms Desola died from, including a shrunken brain and, more grotesquely, the peeling face. These were consequences of the toxic compounds in the fungus. What's more the article was about the discovery of the fungus in Redlynch, Cairns: exactly where the couple had been on holiday a few months earlier. Andre must have found a sample. He certainly had the knowledge of how to sample and cultivate such a fungus.

The case seemed to be coming together at last. Brad phoned Samantha to give her the news.

"Poison fire coral? I think it got mentioned once when I was studying, but we don't have that in Australia do we? I feel like it was mentioned in regards to Japan."

"Apparently a few have been spotted in Queensland, right where they went on holiday a couple of months ago."

"You know, this country gets such a bad rap for how venomous and deadly our wildlife is, but people overlook that our flora is just as bad, like that gympie-gympie case a couple of years ago. That made poison ivy look like a joke."

Brad laughed. "Yes, Australia will be the boss level when the aliens come."

"I'll run some more pathology and see if I can detect the mushroom's toxins. I'm still at work catching up on paperwork. I'll see what I can run now. It might take a while though."

"I'd appreciate it. It's just occurred to me that we haven't flagged Andre's passport. I'll do that."

"Flight risk?"

"Dunno, doesn't seem like it, but then he's wealthy enough to be able to disappear overseas, despite crying poor to us."

"I'll do the tests personally, right now. Speak soon."

~

After filling in Sally on the developments, Brad headed home for dinner with his wife, Amy.

He caught her staring at him and put down his fork. "I know, I'm on edge. It's not about you. It's the potential for an arrest tonight that has me excited."

"At least eat your dinner. That took me ages to make, even though I don't think I could stomach it right now."

"How bad is it?"

"It's not just nausea. I vomited twice this morning. Once was after I did a super stinky fart. The smell triggered me and I threw up breakfast."

Brad laughed.

"You better hope you get that call. 'Cos being amused by my morning sickness will not work out well for you."

"I know, but that was funny. Vomiting because your own fart smelled so disgusting."

Brad's phone rang and he leapt up to answer it.

"Uh huh, yes. Okay, great work." He disconnected the call.

"That was Sam. We have the evidence we need to arrest the husband."

"Go. No coming back all hyped up either. Go get a drink with Sally or something."

"You don't mind?"

Amy laughed. "No. You know I trust you, and you've taught me enough to dispose of you both without being caught if you stray, so we're good."

"I meant given you're sick."

Amy nodded and giggled. "I know."

~

Brad called Sally and let her know they had the information they were waiting on. "Can't say I'm happy about having to come back on duty, but it's our arrest, and I'll be damned if I let anyone else take it," she said.

They found Andre at home, and to Brad's surprise he didn't resist. "I know how it looks against me. When I've spoken to my lawyer, I'll talk. But please know I've been set up."

Brad felt the usual surge of adrenaline an arrest brought. It was always such a rush to declare someone now under police control for a suspected crime.

After Andre was processed and put in a temporary cell, Brad asked Sally out for a drink to celebrate.

"Can't. I have a date with my TV in half an hour. It's down to the last few girls, and one's going home tonight. If I leave now, I'll make it. Try Sam."

Brad called Samantha. "Good idea," she said. "I'm about done here and could use a wind down.

~

Brad met Samantha at an Irish pub in Leederville.

They managed to find a vacant booth and, after a celebratory toast, each took a sip of their beers.

"This was a cracker of a case, you know. It got me thinking," Samantha said.

"Oh yeah. Must be a new experience for you."

Samantha started to raise her middle finger but stopped part way through.

"It got me thinking. How would you kill someone and get away with it? I couldn't get over how stupid it was of Andre to do it in a way which, if discovered, pointed to him."

Brad gave a coy expression.

"Oh, come on. You've investigated, what, dozens or maybe even hundreds of murders? You're saying it's never crossed your mind? I don't believe it."

"Apple seeds," Brad said after a pause.

"Huh?"

"Food is the easiest way to get someone to consume something fatal, and it's much less messy than violence. I'd get two hundred apple seeds and feed them to my victim. The cyanide would kill them in a few hours to a day. Plenty of time for me to get away. Better yet, sneak it onto their desk as a free sample or get a pawn to give it to them without realising what it was. It'd been near impossible to trace."

"Why would they eat apple seeds?"

"'Cos I'd put it in a fruit filled cookie or something."

"But they'd never get the cyanide from the heart of the seed. The husk of the seed would protect them," Samantha said.

"I know." Brad paused and waited until Samantha was looking at him with an exasperated expression. "I'd run the seeds through a coffee grinder. A rinse and bleach of the grinder would get rid of the evidence, especially after refilling it with coffee. I had thought about trying to hide the seed powder in a wheatgrass shot, but then I realised how sludgy the drink would be. So, I'd make it into a paste and inject it into a cookie small enough to eat in one bite."

Samantha laughed. "Remind me not to cross you. But I can tell you've really thought about it. That's not off the top of your head. Anyone in particular you've daydreamt about? An ex or crim who got away perhaps?"

"I'll plead the fifth on that. It was a one-time flight of fancy."

"We don't have the fifth," Samantha protested.

"No comment. What about you?"

Samantha smiled enigmatically. "There is nothing non-toxic, it's only the dose which makes it so. I'd simply strengthen the purity of a medication the person was taking. I'd change the dose in a whole pack of medication so it would seem like a manufacturing mishap, but again, like yours, almost impossible to trace back to me. I'd probably have to make it so it would be a cumulative overdose. They'd never know it was their medicine killing them. With luck, they'd take extra because they were feeling bad."

Samantha stared at her fingers.

"Kids aren't likely to take regular medicine, so you're

clearly thinking of a middle-aged or older person."

Samantha shrugged and continued to look at her hands. She replied absently, "Who'd want to kill a kid?"

"What's up?"

"My fingers are … my index finger is irritated."

"Okay."

"Remember how my glove was torn?"

"Yes."

"Well, the fungus we tested is the only one known to cause skin inflammation on contact."

"If you say so."

"Did you notice any irritation on Andre's hands?"

"No, but he could've worn gloves."

"I don't think you'd miss it if it was there; you're pretty sharp about such things. The thing is, Desola's hands did show irritation. I remember making a note of it on her report," Samantha said.

"She must have handled the mushroom."

"Yes. But then in order to kill her, she'd have to be tricked into touching and eating it. That seems unlikely. Just looking at it, it says don't eat me."

"I see where you're going with this. If you really hated someone, what lengths would you go to for revenge," Brad replied. "Do you know the story of Psyche? She wanted to die after her sisters ruined her life, but was determined to get revenge first. She tricked each into killing themselves, then headed to the underworld to die. We've already discussed how we'd go about it, but what if instead of wanting to end your enemy's life you chose to ruin it instead? I mean if they have to suffer for the remainder of their life, surely that is the most severe revenge, even if it does come at the cost of your own life."

"Getting your enemy convicted of your murder would be pretty brutal revenge."

"Desola had very few friends and was living a dull life. Her husband couldn't bear to be with her and wanted her gone. That was known. Plant a suggestion here and there to make sure people know he wanted her out of his life, say by paying your cleaner to talk to you. The money would make it more memorable," Brad said. "Work out a way of killing yourself which would point to him. Add a bookmark to the relevant page on his computer, something he'd be unlikely to notice. Now you've given probable cause."

"Plant a fungus in his greenhouse when you know he'll be away for a few days and then do the deed."

"Exactly. She'd have to wait for then otherwise he might have forced her to get treatment." Brad smacked his head. "What green thumb would plant mushrooms in a sunny spot? I'm such an idiot. How'd I miss that?"

"But where would she grow it? In this scenario, she placed a grown one in the greenhouse after he left, because he would surely notice it otherwise."

"You could grow one anywhere. All you'd need is soil, shade and moisture."

"You don't need soil. Hydroponics, like what he had on the benches, don't use it," Samantha said.

"One of the setups looked new. I remember thinking

how spotlessly shiny it was."

"If you wanted one for yourself, but also to not be caught ordering it, what would you do?"

"Remove a piece from one of your husbands. Say you'll take it to the tip, then replace the part you took. Now you have a functional setup, without the record of you purchasing one."

"But where would she put it?"

"It couldn't be at the house. We'd have discovered it," Brad said.

"Unless she threw it out beforehand."

"She couldn't go to the tip. There would be cameras monitoring them, and using her own rubbish bin seems unlikely." Brad shook his head. "Oh man, I've been an idiot on this case. The bowling club. That's where it'll be. It was the only other place she was known to go."

"Do they do night bowls? Maybe we could go take a look?"

"I think we'd better get a warrant. Not that I think anyone will be contesting our findings in this case, but just for the club's sake. It is protocol since I'm imagining places not in the public domain will need to be unlocked. It'll have to wait until the morning. I'll write up the paperwork and get it to the magistrate's court tonight. Hopefully, we'll get it back by mid-morning."

Samantha seemed lost in thought.

"What is it?"

"There was something about liquid culture in one of the articles I read about the fungus. I can't quite remember what it was, but look for a bottle of the stuff. It's shelf stable for over half a year, so she may have some with the hydroponics. If she got the specimen a couple of months ago, she'd have needed to replace it a few times."

"I'll look out for it."

~

Brad failed to keep his promise to return home in a calm mood and spent the night tossing and turning as he thought over the case. He couldn't rid himself of the thought of Andre being in a cell, when he might be innocent. That must be a nightmare. Andre had clearly guessed Desola had made it look like he'd done her in, but was smart enough to know the story would sound unbelievable. That's why he was waiting for his lawyer.

Almost as soon as the sun's rays penetrated the curtains, Brad rose and got ready for work, even though his shift wouldn't start for a couple of hours. He scribbled an apology to Amy and left for the bowls club.

He was on his second lap of the track bordering Lake Monger when Sally called. They arranged to meet at the club. It took another lap before the message with their warrant came through, by which time Sally had arrived. Brad was thankful a digital copy would suffice.

Being high up the in the bowls club ranking, Desola had keys to the building. Brad knew the club would be open by ten when the first of the day's bowlers would hit the green. Seeing inside a clubhouse he'd jogged past numerous times before was something he was looking forward to. The trees around the outside of the club had always kept it well hidden, so it would be interesting to see behind the hedge.

The president of the club was the first to arrive. His surprise at two official looking people approaching him as he got out of his car was apparent. "Can I help you?" asked the tall, thin, silver haired man.

"Yes. I'm Sergeant Brad Thomas and this is Detective Sally Summers. We have a warrant to look around your clubhouse. Would that be okay with you?"

The last phrase was just a courtesy. The president had no legal right of refusal. Thankfully, he welcomed them in. As he unlocked the door, he asked what their visit was about. Had they heard they'd been watering down the drinks?

Brad laughed. "No, sir. We'd like to know if perhaps there's a storage area or room only the club secretary had access to?"

"Desola? Why? What's that miserable woman got to do with anything?"

"She, uh, passed away three days ago. We're looking for something she may have left here, which might help us with our enquiries."

"Really! Did she finally do herself in?"

The surprise must have been clear on Brad and Sally's faces.

"My comment before about her being a miserable woman wasn't meant to be sexist, but I can hear how it might seem so. It's just that she was so melancholic a woman we'd dubbed her young misery guts. She was nice enough though, but seemed to be involved with the club just to get out of the house and not for any interest in the sport."

Brad and Sally exchanged glances.

"There is a cupboard behind the bar to which only she and I have access. She did mention once something about storing some papers there. I told her whatever it was would probably turn to dust in there. I don't think I've ever opened it."

Brad's pulse accelerated. That had to be where something revelatory would be hidden.

The president led them round several worn laminate tables to the wood-panelled bar. He lifted a section of the countertop and opened a gate to let them behind it.

He pointed. "It's the bottom one in that corner, next to the bar fridge. I'll open it for you."

It took over two minutes to open as the massive jumble of keys on the keyring were tried one by one. Brad felt himself holding his breath. When at last the president gave a cry of exaltation, Brad practically snorted his breath out. The cupboard was really more of a large filing cabinet drawer. There was a stack of paper right against the edge of a shelf, which ran from the base to the top. Brad took one look at it and laughed. That was not how people stacked things – they would leave room at the top or have something bulky at the top for easy removal. Sally beat Brad to the papers and started passing handfuls of them.

Within a few moments the large pile had diminished enough to see there was something behind it. By the time all the papers were out, it was clear the hidden object was a hydroponic kit. Sally tugged at it to pull it out. "It's stuck, no wait, it's still plugged in!"

Brad manoeuvred the bar fridge out of its spot and unplugged the hydroponic device. After repositioning the fridge he was able to get a close look at what they'd discovered. It certainly had the appearance of the other devices he'd seen in the greenhouse, so Brad and Samantha's theory of its origins seemed accurate. The switch on the side indicated it was turned off. The kit still had a reddish-brown growth culture in its base. The liquid was turbid, but that seemed to be due in part to the bright red fungal bodies growing in it. The spores from the transplanted sample must have grown in the darkness.

It wasn't hard to imagine that if the discovery hadn't been made for a year or two, all that would have been found was a dried reddish coating on the device. If anyone did anything other than thoughtlessly throw out the device at that point, it would be a surprise.

Brad left the clubhouse to call Samantha and discuss what they'd found. "Well, actually, I might have a final confirmation for Andre's innocence, but it would depend on two things," she said. "The first was whether the sample from the greenhouse was planted in soil, and two if the kit you've found used liquid culture. If you could drop me a sample from the kit ASAP I'll get on it."

On his way back into the clubhouse Brad passed the club president who seemed keen to greet the first players as they arrived. Some hot gossip seemed to make him extra fired up to say hello. Brad looked sheepishly at Sally. "I think I made a big mistake arresting Andre. Sam thinks she may be able to prove it wasn't him."

"His lawyer is due to meet with him and us at noon. Do you think you'd be certain by then?"

"I can try. I'll take this sample to Sam right away. Can you finish the bag and tagging and get *El Presidente* to sign an account of what just happened?"

"Yep. That'll take a bit. Hopefully, we can meet back at the station by 11.30 am for a quick debrief before we meet with Andre and his lawyer."

"Despite there being enough evidence to arrest Andre, this seems like it was a suicide dressed up as murder. The opposite of what we might usually suspect."

"All brought about by poison fire. An *apropos* tool for such a devilish plot."

"*Apropos*?" Brad queried.

"What can I say? Your quest for self-improvement is rubbing off. I'm trying to improve my vocabulary."

~

Brad went straight to the morgue to see Samantha. She was in the pathology lab, which was separated from the dissecting rooms by a short corridor. She wasn't bent over a microscope as he'd half-expected, instead she was standing near large box-like machine. She had a thin glass tube lying on the bench. As Brad approached with the sample bag in hand, she said, "Ah good, just what I've been waiting for. Give me a few minutes to prepare a sample, then I'll run an NMR and get a result for you. It'll take about twenty-five minutes all up."

Brad looked at the clock above the bench. That would take them to just after eleven. It would be a close call to get back in time.

"I'm looking for trichothecenes and already have a sample from Desola's blood ready to run to see if they're there too. If they are, it would be conclusive that the mushrooms which killed her were grown hydroponically and came from that batch rather than one grown in soil. That's because the fungus only produces that class of chemical when grown in culture. They're really deadly compounds too. Specifically, I'm hoping the results will show roridin E and satratoxin H. Half a milligram injected into a mouse will kill it within twenty-four hours."

"What can I do?"

"Watch quietly?"

Brad understood this was not his element. Waiting wasn't his strong suit either, and he was soon tapping his foot in anticipation.

"Can you play a game on your phone or something? This needs to be precisely calibrated."

Brad stopped tapping his foot and followed the instruction, though he chose to read the motoring section of the newspaper, in lieu of a game.

A few minutes later, he looked up to see Samantha in front of him. "Coffee?" she asked. "It'll take twenty-ish to run."

Brad suddenly noticed the whirring noise in the room.

"No coffee for me. I'm already wired. Maybe a water?"

"Done."

They finished their drinks and held a conversation about how they could coax Amy into joining them for a run rather than taking their exercise as an opportunity for quiet time alone for herself. The apparatus dinged; its analysis complete. Samantha strode to the machine and sent a few pages to the printer. After comparing them to some other graphs already on her bench, she turned to Brad triumphantly.

"Trichothecenes were found in the sample from the bowls club."

"And the sample of Desola's blood?" Brad asked with bated breath.

"Had them too. I don't know whether to be excited or sorry for her. She must've been so terribly sad to do this to herself."

"Sad is one thing, but she was vengeful. Remember this was done to set up her husband and damn near succeeded. Can I get those reports?"

"Here take these. By the time you get to the station I should have emailed you a proper written report. Thankfully, these days, such things are template-based and don't take long to produce."

"Awesome. Thanks, Sam. You've just saved the remainder of someone's life."

Brad practically skipped to his car.

~

On the drive to the station, Brad's excitement was replaced by worry Andre might sue for wrongful arrest. He certainly had the grounds to make life difficult for Brad, even though any such suit would be dismissed. After all, the initial findings did point to Andre as a killer.

Andre's lawyer was annoyingly early and already at the station when Brad arrived. The overweight man couldn't have been any older than Brad, but he seemed a lot less worldly. His first comments were full of bluster.

"Why are you holding my client? I demand you either charge him or release him immediately."

Brad tried not to laugh. "How often has such a demand worked?"

The lawyer took a step back, then broke into a broad grin. "Not that often, but the drama of it is fun."

"Well, today's your lucky day. I'm happy to release him right now."

The shock was evident on the lawyer's face.

"Shall we go tell him the good news together?"

The lawyer nodded. When they arrived at the cell, Brad was surprised by the transformation in Andre. A single night in prison had turned him from someone who was treating the situation as a surreal dream, to one who was overwhelmed by the seriousness of his circumstance.

"Andre, I am so sorry. I hope you can understand why we detained you."

Andre nodded.

"When you said you were set up, I must confess I didn't believe you, but when my colleagues and I went through the evidence again we began to see cracks in the case. I'm not happy to say your wife killed herself to get back at you, but that's what seems to have happened."

"I knew it. I bloody knew it," Andre exclaimed.

"So, we're letting you go. A full report is being prepared so you can obtain the body from the morgue for a funeral. You were still her next of kin, so it will become your responsibility."

"I'll throw it in the trash."

"No, you won't," Brad said with sudden authority and anger within. "She may have wronged you, but it wasn't entirely without cause. You could have made the childlessness less of an issue between yourselves. You need to make sure she gets a proper dignified send off."

Andre looked suitably chastened. "Fine," he said after a pause.

"You're free to go. The clerk will sort out the return of your things."

Brad turned and left without another word. He couldn't explain why he'd become angry when he'd just been saved from a serious mistake, but something about Andre's instant dismissal of concern over his wife's body irked Brad, and he was pleased to see Andre walk out of the station a few minutes later.

~

That night Brad and Amy sat in a bath, facing each other.

"Ames, what will you do if we can't have kids?"

Amy laughed. "Have you forgotten I'm pregnant?"

"No," Brad maintained his seriousness, "but what if? I've just seen how much it could ruin a couple's life and it worries me it could happen to us."

"We'd get through it. *We* are *not* that couple. Like our friend, Doc, says, it's not the two of us against each other, it's the two of us versus the problem."

"Let's agree to remember that when the baby comes," Brad said.

Amy grinned. "Oh, don't worry, I will."

Brad knew she was being truthful.

The Unique Vision of Mr Kallang

Brad decided the wood panels of the courtroom were an anachronism. The court was only a few years old, well past the century where such flourishes were in vogue. Still, they gave the impression of history and justice being meted out over centuries. However, the LED lighting undid the effect somewhat.

Brad disliked being grilled by defence lawyers trying to pick apart every step of an investigation in an attempt to make a hole open up. In fact, it was the only thing he hated more than paperwork. Most of the time he was certain the defendant had committed the crime, so found the questioning slightly offensive, and the adversarial nature of the conversation meant he had to work very hard to control his temper, something which was emotionally draining.

This case at least had a distinguishing feature which made it unique: no other drug bust had occurred based on the way this particular lab had been discovered.

Brad had been first to testify. Fran Peters, the

prosecutor for this trial, had taken him through his evidence. Brad had always found her to be thoroughly professional and she seemed genuinely interested if the defendant was guilty or not. Her lavender-coloured blazer and matching calf-length skirt weren't the most striking thing about her. That honour belonged to her silver hair. She was the only person Brad knew who dyed her hair silver for the aesthetic of it, despite, at thirty-five years of age, it not being her natural hair colour. The effect, combined with her measured speech, was such that she took on a mystical quality. She appeared wiser, calmer and more honest than her peers, especially in contrast to her adversary in this trial, Percy Sutton. Brad had been cross-examined by him before, and found him to be somewhat full of himself, but cunningly smart when it came to picking holes in testimony.

Brad told the jury how he'd been at the front desk of the police station, talking to a senior constable, when Mark Kallang called into the police station after taking a walk. Mark said he'd noticed a massive amount of UV light coming from a building. In his mind, the only thing that would generate that from inside a building would be either a tanning bed salon or drug lab. In either case, both were illegal.

Brad didn't state it in the court, as it wasn't his place to explain Mark's ability, but he'd pressed him on it at the time. Mark's claim was incredible, but scientifically viable. He could see into the UV range of the electromagnetic spectrum. A year ago, he'd had experimental cataract surgery. A surgeon had had recent success performing two lens replacements in the one surgery and Mark was his final guinea pig before he was due to write a paper on the process. Two custom toric lenses had been made for insertion into Mark's eyes after his cloudy lenses were removed. The surgeon started with the right eye, but when it came to implanting the lens it was dropped, then trodden on in the search for it. Since its bespoke nature meant no replacement was available, it was decided to leave the eye without a lens temporarily and schedule another appointment to insert one. Mark had been conscious during the mishap and said it was okay for them to proceed to the other eye, though he would have scowled had his eyes not been clamped and nerves numbed by local anaesthetic. At least he'd still have improved vision in one eye, which would allow him to watch over his grandkids with more ability to look out for their welfare.

It hadn't taken long to regret his decision. In a near re-enactment of the first accident, the second lens was also dropped, though this time by the assisting nurse rather than the surgeon. The surgeon apologised profusely, fixed each eye as would normally occur and asked Mark to come back the following month when his eyes had healed enough for the procedure to be repeated.

Mark had been driven home by his granddaughter, who had been reluctant to leave him on his own, but Mark assured her he'd be okay and could actually see better than before. "The clouds have lifted."

Without his lenses, Mark's close-up vision was blurry,

but after shifting the couch further back from the TV and switching to audiobooks, within a few days he hardly noticed his disability. That was until he became concerned by the whitish-purple tinges he kept seeing. It was only when he looked at a brightly coloured flower in his garden and saw patterns which weren't there previously, he twigged he was seeing ultra-violet light. After that revelation, his panic subsided, and Mark began to enjoy seeing the world in this new way. By the end of the month, he found himself delaying the next appointment. The lure of wanting to experience the world in this new way for a little longer was too much. Weeks turned into months, and it had now been over a year since his botched surgery. Strong glasses helped with close-up vision, and he'd already given up driving before the cataract surgery, so Mark found himself able to cope without too much inconvenience.

The perspective shift was something Brad related to, since a few years before when he'd worked through a program to improve his thought processes. He enjoyed his new way of thinking about things despite its one drawback of no longer being able to let even mundane things be simple. A sunset wasn't just an aesthetically pleasing image and array of colours, but had to be appreciated for the scattering of different wavelengths of light and gravitational lensing of the sun's rays. That too had to be appreciated for briefly making the sun still visible even when it had passed below the horizon.

Brad testified that after the tip off he'd walked the street a few times in plain clothes and noticed several people enter and exit the building within a few minutes. They all looked around when they left, as though concerned they were being observed. Brad thought he recognised one of them as someone he'd written up for a drug related misdemeanour a few months earlier. He'd applied for, and been granted, a warrant to search the house.

"What happened next?" Fran asked Brad, though she was looking at the jury. The effect was of confidence the testimony would be damning.

"We assembled a small team and proceeded to the property. I knocked on the door, which the defendant opened. I explained our purpose was to have a look around due to a suspicion of drug manufacturing occurring on the premises. The defendant asked to see the warrant, which I showed him. He read it, said 'okay' and held the door for us to enter the building. The moment the last officer had crossed the threshold, he made a run for it out the front door, slamming it shut behind him."

"And then?"

"The senior constable opened the door and ran after him. He caught him pretty quickly. I'd say within a couple of hundred metres from the building. He returned the defendant cuffed and out of breath."

"What did you find inside the building?"

"That was where it was interesting. It was one of those warehouse conversions, so ostensibly it was a home, but most of the interior was, in effect, one big drug lab. At the front of the building, where Mr Kallang had seen the UV light, there was a substantial poppy farm, under UV lights. On a mezzanine level, a large volume of chemical equipment was present, as well as what we later weighed to be 2.3 kilograms of heroin."

"The prosecution would like to enter into evidence photographs a to i of this case, depicting what the witness is describing."

"Proceed," the judge replied. Her voice was authoritative.

Fran placed a series of A1 sized boards with images from the crime scene onto easels. Brad made sure to stop his mouth twitching into a smile. She always used that size, while most of her peers used A2. Brad speculated she felt the larger size made an equally larger impression.

"Is this what you found?" Fran asked.

"Yes, though I'm not sure the pictures adequately show the extent of the operation."

Fran couldn't stop a smile spreading over her face. Brad knew such statements were like gold for prosecutors.

"This was a very major operation. The quantity we busted them with had a street value of about $800,000. They were producing that amount several times per year. The purity of their product was higher than the usual maximum percentage of 68%. We suspected several dozen recent overdoses could be attributed directly to their product—"

"Objection, speculation," Percy interrupted.

"Sustained. Please keep your answers to the question you've been asked," the judge admonished, while shaking her head.

Brad nodded. "We examined leasing records and the defendant was renting the property. Similarly, our forensic accounting team were able to show he was living well above his means and had unexplained income."

"Objection. It's not this witnesses place to talk about income," Percy said.

"Sustained. Sergeant Thomas, you will restrict your testimony to actions you were directly involved with," the judge said.

"Yes, Your Honour. There isn't much more to report. We have affidavits, which I collected from several users who admit buying heroin from that location and from the defendant specifically."

"So, in terms of charging the client how strong would you say your case is?" Fran asked.

"Objection, calls for speculation," Percy immediately replied.

The judge directed his reply to Brad. "Overruled, but please keep your answer based on evidence not intuition."

"Okay. We found clear evidence of heroin manufacturing on the premises, which was in the defendant's name, and further he was found at the location at the time of the raid. He knew it was occurring there. We obtained the sworn statements that the defendant was dealing from that location. The defendant's financial records indicate the dealing had been occurring for some time. I've rarely had a case so straightforward. I'd be happy to present this case to a jury anywhere in the world."

Brad meant what he said. Even Percy must know he was defending a guilty man.

"Thank you. No further questions, Your Honour," Fran said.

"Cross?" the judge asked Percy.

"I'd be delighted," Percy replied.

How could Percy be comfortable trying to free his client? It was contrary to justice. Brad remembered an interviewer asking a well-known QC how he could defend 'someone who you yourself believe not to be innocent' and the response was, 'Well, they're the best cases. I mean, you really feel you've done something when you get the guilty off. Anyone can get an innocent person off. I mean, they shouldn't be on trial. But the guilty, that's the challenge.' Was that how Percy saw this? A challenge? How could he deny the evidence presented?

~

Percy began to pace from one side of the jury to the other, as though vexed.

"Ladies and gentlemen of the jury, what we have heard from Sergeant Thomas is, despite his claims, nothing more than circumstantial evidence."

Brad couldn't hide his bemusement. The statement was preposterous. Percy suddenly turned on his heels and practically barked his question at Brad. "Was the suspected drug user you'd seen present at the time of the raid?"

"No," Brad replied without hesitation.

"If he wasn't there, how can you be certain you'd seen a known drug addict enter the premises?"

Brad tried not to scowl. It didn't take a law degree to know where Percy was going with his cross-examination. He was going to challenge the validity of the warrant. If the procedure for the issue and execution of the search warrant had not been properly followed, then the court could rule it was invalid. If that occurred, then the evidence collected would be inadmissible and the case against the drug dealer would collapse. The dealer would be free before lunchtime. It was the basic rule of defence law: if the facts are against you, argue the law, and if the law is against you then attack the person. The thing Brad was reluctant to admit was that the gang responsible for the drugs hadn't been on the police's radar. It was a fluke they'd been discovered, and he was afraid they'd soon relocate and be equally as unknown.

"I can't be a hundred percent certain it was him, but I'm good at recognising people and am confident it was."

"But not certain."

"I've already said that."

"Who did you get the warrant from? The local magistrate?"

Brad forced himself to smile, instead of giving Percy the angry glare he wanted to. Percy knew the answer full well.

"No, I had a local justice of the peace issued the warrant. It was more expedient, and we wanted to catch the group in the act."

"A justice of the peace and not a judge? That seems unusual."

Brad couldn't stop his brow creasing at the comment. It was clear Percy was trying to make it seem the warrant and justification for it were unusual and based on flimsy evidence.

"Not at all. JPs are an important part of the legal system. Their warrants are as valid as any other."

"Only if the underlying evidence they're based on is real," Percy retorted.

Brad was further annoyed to see, through his peripheral vision, several jury members nod at the comment.

"You think the heroin wasn't real?" Brad asked.

"It may have been, but I'm referring to your interpretation of the defendant's presence at the location at the time of your raid. I put it to you he had no idea what was going on at the premises when you arrived. He had been misled by a friend who was using the property and had just discovered the betrayal when you arrived. Naturally, he panicked, so he ran."

"And the financial records?"

"Some wins at the casino are hardly illegal. However, coercing witnesses to identify a suspect is."

Brad tried to think of the word for the emotion he was feeling. *Flabbergasted.* That was it. "Objection. Your Honour, such a comment is in contempt of court," Fran interjected. It was too late; the damage from the comment was already visible on the faces of the jury.

"I withdraw the comment. No further questions."

The judge dismissed Brad as a witness. Brad sat in the gallery and observed the trial. He should really head back to his station, but in the last week both Detective Summers and he had solved significant cases, so he was due for a lighter day. What better way than seeing a suspect actually declared guilty for a change? – assuming the jury didn't fall for Percy's bluster.

~

Fran guided the next witness, Mr Kallang, through his discovery of the drug lab. Mr Kallang's sincerity had a good impression on the jury. As his statement neared its end, Brad noticed Percy practically chomping at the bit to cross-examine. It seemed like an act, but one which, if the jury were paying attention, would serve to help them question what they felt was true. Percy jumped out of his chair and strode right up to the witness box.

"Mr Kallang, can you please explain, for the court, how it is you were able to tell the building on Palmerston Street was a drug lab just by walking past it?" Percy asked in formal tones.

From his vantage point about seven metres from the witness box, Brad could see – thanks to Mr Kallang's thick convex glasses – that Mark's relatively small pupils dilated just enough to be noticeable, but only because he was looking for it. Good. He was preparing to defend himself.

"I was walking along the street to—" Mark began.

"Were you wearing the glasses you are now?" Percy interrupted.

"No."

"So how can we believe you could see anything?"

"I have aphakia," Mark said quietly.

"Excuse me?"

"I have aphakia," Mark said more confidently.

"This is inexcusable, Your Honour. Please find the witness in contempt," Percy said indignantly.

The judge cleared her throat to reply.

Mr Kallang scrunched his face, then just as quickly his features relaxed. "Oh, you think I'm swearing. No. There's a disorder I suffer from. It's 'a' for absence, 'phak' as in phakos, meaning lens, and '–ia' as in hyperopia. Put it together and you have a disorder called aphakia."

"Please stop saying that," Percy said.

"It means I don't have lenses in my eyes. It's why I'm so far-sighted. I also can't accommodate properly, which means I struggle with depth perception."

"You don't have lenses? And you were walking around without glasses," Percy said, mirroring the confusion on the faces of the jury.

Such imitation of body language was key to getting the jury to feel a connection to his perspective on the case.

"When I take my glasses off, I gain an ability to see into the ultra-violet spectrum. Normally the lenses absorb UV light. Without mine, or my glasses it gets through. I often go for walks through the streets, and also through King's Park, without my glasses. It's just a whole new world."

"Ladies and gentlemen of the jury, putting aside that outrageous claim for the moment, I put it to you that if the prosecution's key witness can't even see your faces without glasses the thickness of coke bottles—"

"You seem to misunderstand the nature of my vision

problem. My distance vision is fine. I can see the jury and courtroom without difficulty. What I couldn't do without my glasses is read something you put in front of me. You're probably thinking of myopia where you can't see distance. That's the opposite of what I have."

Percy scowled, while Brad mentally cheered for Mr Kallang. Being shown up by a witness was probably not something Percy experienced very often.

"So, you were walking along and …?"

"And I saw a glow emanating from a building on Palmerston Street. There are a bunch of warehouse to house conversions there. One had rays of whitish-violet pouring out of any gap in the blinds. There were streaks coming through them like rays of light through a cloud. It was very beautiful."

"Bullshit," Percy said. It wasn't hard to imagine Percy was trying to show he understood the thoughts of the jury, who looked as disbelieving as the prosecutor.

Fran leapt on the indiscretion. "Objection, Your Honour."

"My apologies to the court. That was most unprofessional of me," Percy said with what appeared to be mock sincerity. He failed to suppress a smile. The effect on the jury was exactly what Brad guessed Percy was hoping for. It seemed they agreed with him. Even a sanction from the judge, with the admonition to control himself or be found in contempt, couldn't keep the upturn away from the edges of Percy's mouth.

"Am I allowed to ask something?" Mark asked the

judge.

"No," said the judge.

"I mean about procedure."

"You may ask about your rights, that is all," the judge replied.

"Okay … well, then let me say this in response to Mr Sutton's exclamation of a few moments ago. It is not bullshit, it is fact. If you don't believe me put me to the test. I've been a juror before, and we did a 'jury view' of the crime scene. Since my testimony seems crucial, why can't we go outside and I'll show you?"

"Mr Kallang it is not up to a witness to dictate what we do in this courtroom," Percy said, in fatherly but condescending tones.

"However, a demonstration may be worthwhile," said the judge. "But we haven't arranged for a jury view, so we'll have to do one here, in the room. We will have a fifteen-minute recess. In that time I'm sure, Mr Sutton, you can run down to the art supply store, which is a few doors down, and buy an invisible ink pen and some cartridge paper."

"This is most unusual," Percy protested.

"You were the one who challenged the witness," the judge said.

Brad guessed why Percy was going so hard on Mark's testimony. If he could undermine the witness's credibility and make it seem like the basis for the search warrant was invalid, then Percy may be able to get the case dismissed on a technicality.

The court resumed fifteen minutes later. Brad had remained seated when everyone else cleared out, and had snuck a quick text to his station to say he'd be back in a couple of hours. He turned his phone off again afterwards. Being caught with it on while the court was in session was considered contempt.

Towards the end of the recess, it had been interesting to watch Percy reappear and then paint several symbols onto A3 sheets of paper using a pot of 'invisible' paint. Brad was able to tell what the symbols were by watching the motion of the brush. He'd started with an ampersand, then *pi* and the number seven. The last two were a smiley face and a triangle. All relatively unambiguous. Percy numbered each page with a pen and wrote down what each symbol was on a separate piece of paper. It seemed a fair test. Percy draped the images over Fran's easels – *literally covering the evidence* – Brad shook his head at the gall of the lawyer.

Once everyone was settled back into the courtroom, Mark immediately stared at the first sheet of paper, took off his glasses, then after a moment looked bemused. Brad smiled. This would cement the case against the defendant.

"I've painted five symbols on the pieces of paper. Can you tell me what they are?"

Mark appeared embarrassed and looked from Fran to Brad and back again. An unexpected sense of dread settled over Brad.

"I'm sorry, no, I can't. Are you trying to trick me?

There's nothing on them."

Brad's mind flashed through the whole case. Had he been duped into raiding the building? Why would that even matter, since a large amount of heroin was found there? The rest of the evidence was strong. The case was strong. But what had the warrant said? Brad tried to recall the wording.

Percy couldn't have looked more delighted. He immediately called for a mistrial.

"I'll need to read the warrant and consider the legality of it before I rule on your request, Mr Sutton. There will be another fifteen-minute recess." She nodded, then stood and walked to her chamber.

Brad started a timer on his watch and raced out of the room to use his phone. The phone seemed to take an eternity to turn back on. Brad watched the seconds go by on the timer. Once the phone was operational, Brad called the one person he thought could help him.

"Doc, I need your help," Brad said to his mentor and semi-secret weapon, Dr Engels. Dr Engels was a biotech entrepreneur.

"My dear boy, that's a bit dramatic don't you think?" Dr Engels said jovially.

"I've got thirteen minutes to figure out why someone who previously has been able to see into the ultra-violet spectrum suddenly isn't able to anymore. Otherwise, a drug dealer will go free and people will die."

"That's quite the deadline. Tell me everything and I'll help if I can."

"A witness who has aphakia and could see UV light couldn't just now in the courtroom."

"I'm not familiar with that disorder. I'm guessing he's missing something?"

"The lenses in his eyes. I looked it up. The reduced depth of the clear parts of the eye allows UV light into the eye rather than having it filtered out by the cornea and lens. But a demo of the ability in court didn't work."

"Explain the demo to me."

Brad described how images were painted on parchment, but Mr Kallang couldn't identify them.

"That's odd. It's not meant to be something you can switch off."

"I know. But if they can make it seem like he doesn't have the ability, they'll invalidate the warrant, and our case falls apart."

"Hold on. I'm thinking."

Brad looked at his watch. Eleven minutes to go.

"The ink they used. Was it lemon-based or something else?"

"I don't think it was lemon juice. It was definitely one that glows under a UV torch."

"Damn, that was going to be my solution."

Brad involuntarily held his breath while waiting for his mentor to continue. After half a minute he consciously exhaled. "Nine minutes."

"Sorry, I can't think of anything else. The ink you described reflects UV light. It should be visible to your witness. Describe the room to me. Maybe that'll reveal something?"

"It's a courtroom at the new district court building."

"I've settled some civil matters there," Dr Engels said dryly. "Which courtroom were you in?"

"Number five. The middle room on the fourth floor."

"Not a room with windows?" Dr Engels voice rose, causing Brad's heart to pound.

"No, no windows."

Dr Engels sighed. "Ah … no, wait. Damn, I thought I was on to something, you know, by questioning the assumption of the question. In this case that there was UV light to reflect." Brad's hope waned. "Because, as you know, in order for UV light to be reflected off something there must be a source of it. I was about to say you had no source, but then I remembered fluorescent lights give off UV."

"The lighting is LED, not fluorescent."

"There's your answer. LEDs don't give off UV. For your witness to be able to see UV light there needs to be a source of it." Brad felt his heart start thumping again. "Get him to give the same demo outside."

"You're a genius. Thank you."

Dr Engel's laughed. "I've been called worse."

~

Brad had six minutes left to find Fran. He ran back into the courtroom, but she wasn't there. She wouldn't have time to get coffee, so where would she go when needing to think about something quietly? *The toilet.* Brad ran to them. Outside the women's restroom he paused briefly, took a breath and strode into the room. He got a dirty look from a woman leaving, but she didn't say anything. Brad raced past the sinks and hand dryers into the area with the toilet stalls. "Fran?" he called out.

"Go away," a voice replied.

"Fran, I know why Mark couldn't see the symbols. There was no UV light in the room. LEDs don't give it off. He'll be able to see them if you get him to view the images where there's daylight."

"What?"

"You've got to convince the judge to let you show Mark the images outside."

"Hang on." A toilet flushed, and a moment let Fran came out of her stall. "Sergeant Thomas?" she said after looking him up and down.

"Yes."

"You shouldn't be in here."

"I know, but" – Brad glanced at his watch – "we only have a couple of minutes before we need to be back in the courtroom."

"Okay. Got it. Thanks for the information. I'll do what I can."

~

Brad returned to his seat in the gallery as everyone else filed back into the courtroom.

"I've been asked to consider a mistrial in this case, due to a question over the validity of the warrant," the judge said. She looked annoyed by the development.

"Your Honour, I apologise for interrupting, but I think

there's something you need hear," Fran asserted.

"I doubt it. I'm afraid in reading the warrant, its validity does seem to hinge on Mr Kallang's ability to see UV light as he claims. So, without that, the warrant is invalid and all the evidence collected under it cannot be used by the jury when considering their verdict. No evidence equals no case to answer for. I'm inclined to grant the mistrial."

Percy and the defendant were beaming. Brad was surprised they didn't high five such was their joy.

"Wait. Mr Kallang couldn't see the images because there's no UV light in this courtroom. LEDs don't emit UV light. Show him the images outside. I guarantee he'll be able to see them."

Brad cringed. Guarantee was a very strong word, although in this case it was effective. The judge tilted her head just a fraction.

"Interesting. Okay let's have a jury view in the foyer. Since we're only walking a few metres out of the courtroom, that should be okay."

"Your Honour, don't the windows have UV shield on them?" Fran said.

"Actually, I think they do. All right, we'll make it out to the street. Mr Sutton, please bring your pictures. Bailiff you will escort the defendant."

Percy's buoyancy deflated as the bailiff nodded, and everyone filed out of the room. Brad hoped Percy was thinking his case was about to be sunk.

~

As he stepped out onto the street, Brad raised a hand to

his forehead to shield his eyes from the light. The bright sun was perfect for such as demonstration. A minute later, the judge, legal teams and jury filed out. Mark walked slowly out of the building a moment later. He didn't seem as perturbed by the sun as everyone else. The judge called everyone together on the steps of the building. Brad couldn't take his eyes off Mark as the demonstration started. Percy held up the first piece of paper. Brad didn't see anything on it, but the moment it was turned towards Mark, there was the clear sign of recognition on Mark's face.

"That's an and sign," he said confidently.

"And this?" Percy said as he held up the second sheet.

"Three point one four one five. That's the symbol for *pi*."

Percy held up the successive sheets. "Seven, smiley emoji, triangle."

Percy nodded in response to the judge's questioning glance.

"Well, Mr Sutton, it looks like the warrant was valid after all."

Percy exchanged a few words with his client.

"Your Honour, my client would like to change his plea to guilty."

"Can you confirm that?" the judge asked. The defendant nodded and followed with a clear, "Yes."

"Very well. We'll head back to the courtroom. I'll dismiss the jury and we can proceed from there."

Fran tapped Brad on the elbow. "Thanks for the tip."

"That's okay. I'm glad I stuck around. It was good to see justice served."

"Even if they did just buy themselves a sentence reduction by changing their plea?"

"Sentencing isn't my thing. I'm just pleased he's been stopped. My friends in the medical examiner's office will be too – they've seen too many overdoses recently."

~

Brad drove back to his station, eating a plum along the way. Its sweetness seemed enhanced by the courtroom victory. After checking for cameras, while stopped at a red light, Brad set a reminder in his phone to send Dr Engels a bottle of sloe gin as a thank you. For the remainder of his journey, he kept wondering whether his future child would have any unique abilities like Mr Kallang. What would be something desirable, but not so outstanding that the child would need to be studied?

Froggy

Brad had just started his drive to work one morning, when the service due warning flashed up on his car display. It was perfect timing. It gave him and Amy a perfect excuse to visit his family and share their happy news. He'd just have to okay his sister, Emily, being free to service the car. Amy would also have to be okay with the sudden idea of a weekend away. Leaving during peak hour on Friday would make it a two-hour drive to Northam, so it was far enough away to make staying a night or two worthwhile.

Once Brad had called Amy and got her enthusiastic approval, he called Emily.

"Sure, it'll be great to see you guys. But be warned. Tammy hasn't been given the attention she deserves so far this week. She may be a little excitable when you arrive."

"We can't wait to see her."

"I'll let her know you're coming."

"Any chance you could squeeze my car in for a service on Saturday morning? That's why we want to come."

Emily hesitated. "Petey's got his ute booked in *ah-gain*.

Seriously, he's in every couple of months these days, but yeah sure, I'll squeeze you in. That's what family's for, right?"

"Sure is. Thanks for that. And how are you going?"

"Meh. Losing my job hasn't been as bad as I thought. I'm getting to tinker like I did when we were teens. I enjoy helping Johno, and the downturn doesn't seem to be affecting the garage too much. So, we're coping. We reduced our labour charges on most services and let people know we were doing it to help them out. They seem to have responded by keeping their services up. We're lucky we're not in the city where people can cope without a car more easily. 'Cos they're essential here people are better at maintaining them."

"I'm busy too. Economic downturns certainly see us start to get stretched. There's more petty theft and, worse, many more domestic callouts. On the plus side, the murder rate is holding steady."

"Did you hear about our one?" Emily asked.

"Your one what?"

"Sarge will probably want to talk with you while you're down here. I think he's a bit out of his depth."

"What happened?" Brad persisted.

"Someone poisoned Jimmy. He's dead."

"What? How am I only hearing about this now?"

"It only happened on the weekend, but the whole town's abuzz."

"He was the mayor. Of course they're going to talk," Brad said.

"And a philanderer."

"Yes, he definitely was a womaniser and not a philanthropist who gives money to causes."

"Huh?"

"Just how I remember the difference," Brad said. "I need to say the whole thing to get it right."

"Anyway, someone seems to have poisoned him. That's all I know. Everyone knows poison is a woman's weapon, so they're mentally sorting through all his past girlfriends as suspects. It's quite the topic of conversation. There's even a WhatsApp group where people are discussing who they think it is."

"Which you'd only know if you were part of it."

"You've got me there." Emily laughed. "Pretty sharp, bro."

"I'm thinking faster these days. So, who do you think it is?"

"My money's on Casey. She's so firey. I think she'd go that far."

"You have to choose the one serious girlfriend I had before I moved to the city as your suspect?"

"Well, look at how she treated you."

"I wasn't the same back then."

"No, but she hasn't changed, whereas you have. She's still as domineering as ever."

"She wasn't that bad. She just wasn't afraid to go after something she wanted. Once she felt she had me in her palm, she manipulated me into ending it so she could move on to her next conquest."

"And broke your heart in the process."

"I got over it pretty quickly. It was nearly six years ago; you should too."

"I don't like it when people mess with my little brother."

"Poison wouldn't be her style. Not that I don't think she'd kill someone, but she'd stab or shoot them. Poison would be too indirect."

"So, you've thought about her killing someone?"

"I haven't, no." He didn't want to admit Casey had also been his first thought as a suspect.

"Okay, little brother. I'd better get back to it. See you Friday. Usual time?"

"Yup."

Brad pushed the speed limit for the rest of his trip to the station.

~

Once at work, Brad walked briskly to his office, shut the door, and fired up his laptop. A search for Mayor Jimmy's death revealed a few more details. Jimmy had called the emergency line on Sunday afternoon, complaining he was losing the ability to move and breathe. Brad put in a request for a copy of the call with his regular contact from dispatch. She replied to his email with the file within a few minutes. It wasn't illegal for Brad to ask for the audio file, but it wasn't strictly protocol either.

Jimmy sounded like he was struggling to breathe and speak on the recording. He gasped out the words, "Can't breathe, think dying," and was only just able to say his name, "Jim Shireman." He appeared to have passed out before confirming his location, but as he'd called from a landline phone, it had been straightforward to find him. Brad looked forward to his days off, but his curiosity was so piqued by this mystery in his hometown, he couldn't wait to get stuck into it during their weekend visit.

He headed to the kitchen and ran into his friend, Samantha, the medical examiner. Both were going for the communal pot of coffee.

"What's wrong?" she asked him.

"What do you mean?"

"You haven't asked how I am, or why I'm here and not over at the morgue. Nor did you say 'greetings', which is usually your equivalent of hello."

"Am I that bad?"

"It's endearing but repetitive. Anyway, you've waited for me to pour my mug without a word, ergo something's on your mind."

"Ergo?"

Sam laughed. "Yes, ergo. Now, err, go tell me what's up."

"There was a murder in my hometown. At least it looks that way. The mayor was poisoned."

"And?"

"I know the victim and probably all the suspects personally. I'm trying to figure out who it could be. It bothers me I might be friends with a killer."

"Why?"

"Seems like something I should be able to spot, as in

that's my job."

"You haven't lived in the town for years. People change. They probably weren't killer material when you were there, but could be now."

"Thanks. I think I needed to hear that."

Brad sipped his coffee as he went back to his office. One of his detectives had once told him the habit made him look busy, which only had the effect of making the unconscious habit a conscious one. Brad didn't want to let on that today he had a rare, lighter than usual, workload. He needed time to think. He'd been sitting with his feet up on his desk for a few minutes before he realised he hadn't asked Samantha why she was there. He went back to the kitchen, but she was gone.

~

On his drive home that evening, Brad called his former Sergeant, whom the whole town knew simply as Sarge.

"I'm glad you called," Sarge said after the usual pleasantries. "I was thinking of contacting you about this mess with Mayor Jim. I know these days you're a much better detective than when you were here. Not that I think you city boys are any better than us, just that you've come into your own down there. Besides, you knew Jimmy, know the town, and might be able to see what I can't. 'Cos right now, I'm stumped. He died so quickly that there was no time for him to identify who gave him the poison, even assuming he knew who it was or that he'd been poisoned. We've had a state coroner up to have a look. They're gonna let us know tomorrow what they found."

"I'll be interested to know what they come up with."

"You and me both. Between us, the list of suspects is quite long. Jim annoyed a lot of husbands and scorned a lot of women. My hope is the tox report identifies something to narrow down who it could be."

"Let's hope so. Maybe you'll get lucky and it'll somehow narrow it to a single person. Anyway, I'll be down tomorrow evening. Maybe we could have a drink at Brooke's Pub?" Brad suggested.

"I'll try and get that table for two next to the fire. Should be a little more private."

What would Amy make of the old-fashioned country pub? She hadn't gone to it despite several visits to the town to meet Brad's family. With a start, he realised she shouldn't come along.

"Amy won't be happy she's missing out on a drink with you, but if we're discussing a case she shouldn't be there."

"I'll have to catch up with her another time. See you there at seven?" Sarge asked.

"Better make it half-past. I won't finish here until five, and I'll have to drop Amy at my sister's."

"Not staying with your parents?"

"No."

"But you're talking to them."

"Yes. We'll even have dinner with them on Saturday."

"Good. I'm glad you're functioning better these days."

"Well, Emily and my roles are reversed now. I'm now the big city success, and she's the failure in their eyes."

"I don't know how good she was as a structural

engineer, but can I just say she's a damn fine mechanic and doing wonders for Johno's business. I think her enthusiasm is a pleasant change."

"Good of you to say. It was hard for her to lose her job, but yeah, it might have been the best thing for her. Just don't tell my parents I said that."

Sarge laughed. "Done. See you tomorrow."

~

After a distracted morning, Brad was chomping at the bit to leave for Northam. While it wasn't a locked room mystery, Northam was relatively insular, so the perpetrator was almost certainly a local. Brad likely knew them and that produced conflicting emotions. On one hand, there was the excitement of catching someone who, maybe just maybe, was a person who had picked on or wronged Brad in the past. On the other hand, there was a killer in the town where his parents and sister lived. What if one of them was next? Unfortunately, Amy was taking her time getting ready, despite having a bag which Brad had packed the night before. Amy repacked the case twice, while regularly going to, and staring into, the fridge. Her explanation was that she was concerned she might get a craving for something, so she wasn't sure if she should pack some food.

"Oh, come on. There are shops in the town you know. I'm sure we can get anything you might need," Brad said.

"But they might not stock my brand."

"I don't care, we need to get going," Brad said tersely.

"Don't snap at me," Amy replied. Her face flushed.

72

"This whole situation is new to me. I don't know what to expect."

"Sorry. I'm sorry Ames. This whole hometown murder is bugging me. What if the murderer is someone I know? How could I have not thought them capable of it earlier? What would that say about me? How bad a cop must I be?"

"You haven't been home for ages, at least not for seeing your friends. You've been away for years. Circumstances change. The economy is stuffed due to the mining downturn, and that changes people."

"Thanks." Brad gave Amy a hug. "Sorry," he added.

~

Despite the apology the mood remained tense as they fought through city traffic. Once they were out of the city, Brad forced himself to exhale and try to enjoy the drive.

As they finally were able to accelerate to the freeway's limit, Amy seemed to pick up on Brad's shift in mood. "Why do you call your Northam mates such odd things?" Amy asked softly. "I thought I knew the obvious nicknames for most names, but I can't figure out how, instead of being Pete, Peter is Petey, David isn't Dave, he's Davey, and Johnathan isn't Johnny, he's Johno. Casey isn't shortened at all, and Jim a one-syllable name is extended to Jimmy. You also call Henry, Froggy."

Brad smiled. "There's a trick. Basically, you need to have a two-syllable name which ends on an open sound, preferably a y or an open vowel."

"Why? Doesn't make sense to me."

"Have you heard the word cooee?"

"Yeah. It's like a long-distance shout of hello."

"Pretty much. Distinctly Aussie too. But think about it. To call over distance, with energy, you need something easily recognised and with an 'up' ending for that extra volume and carry. That's why Dave or David don't work they have closed sounds at the end, but Davey works just fine. Froggy is just Froggy because he researches frogs for a living."

Amy smiled.

"So that's how we gave ourselves our nicknames. They work for shouting at each other over a distance."

"Cool, but it does make me realise we're going to have to think a lot more about baby names."

"You're planning on yelling at our child over a distance?"

"Haha."

"We'll get there. Don't worry."

"Hang on, you haven't said what your nickname was, and I don't think you've ever told me," she said.

Brad admired the amusement in Amy's eyes. It was always when he found her the most attractive.

"Nope. Not telling."

~

The approach to Northam made Brad reflect on his upbringing. Northam was located in the Avon Valley, with the Avon River flowing through the town. It was a picturesque country town, which somehow seemed out of place in outback Western Australia. Comparatively recent artificial banks had been added to the river to prevent floods, but historically the town had been devastated by floods a few times and was a mix of older and newer buildings. The townsfolk were fiercely proud that unlike most other inland towns, Northam wasn't based around a mine site. They also boasted Australia's longest pedestrian suspension bridge, which crossed 'their' river. The bridge wasn't particularly high. Brad had jumped from it into the river more than once as a kid. His sister had also been inspired by the bridge and credited it as spurring her interest in structural engineering.

As they reached the backstreets and approached his sister's house, Brad couldn't help but notice how many driveways were simply dirt. It was such a contrast to the city where they were nearly all paved or concreted. Brad couldn't help but think the dirt would be good for capturing footprints or tyre tracks after some rain.

Brad smiled wryly. He'd moved on so much from being in the town. He enjoyed visiting it to reminisce, but had no regrets about moving to the city and enjoying all the opportunities it afforded him. Brad was mildly surprised to realise he hadn't spoken to any of his Northam friends since his wedding just over two years earlier. Not Petey, Davey or Froggy. He'd only spoken to his family and to Sarge a couple of times.

They arrived at Emily's house, a small redbrick with a tin roof and wooden fences. Brad parked in the street and carried their bags to the front door. He rang the doorbell while Amy closed the gate behind them and was immediately greeted by the loud barking of a dog who could be heard tearing her way to the front door. A moment later he heard his sister's voice say, "Tammy, it's just Brad and Amy. I told you they were coming."

Emily opened the door. She was holding a very excited German shepherd by its collar. "I told her you were coming. I don't think it helped."

"Hi, sis. Good to see you. Can you let her go?" He turned to Amy. "She may jump."

"There's no may about it," Emily chimed in, as she let go of Tammy. "And why are you talking as though she's never met Tammy before?"

Amy laughed. "It's all good."

Brad knelt, which didn't stop Tammy from jumping all over the place. Her tail whipped from side to side, and she whined excitedly in between licking Brad's face and trying to sniff Amy.

"Tammy, I've missed you." Brad gave the dog a cuddle and received ear licks and nibbles in response. "Who's a good girl, Tammy?"

He looked at Amy. "I wish we could have a dog in our apartment." It was the thing he missed most about life in the country. Emily moved into the house and held the door for them.

"A dog that big wouldn't fit, and we're not moving to the 'burbs," Amy said in mock warning tones.

Brad sighed and nodded, then followed them all into the house.

~

After settling into the guest room, Brad left his sister's for

Brooke's Pub. The pub was old-fashioned, with a working fireplace and plenty of tables. The one thing it needed was some booths, but otherwise it was a very pleasant country pub. Brad bought an Irish beer, then found Sarge where he said he'd be – next to the fire, sitting at what was probably the most private table in the place. Sarge put down his beer and stood as Brad approached. His heavyset features, grey hair, bushy moustache and tattooed arms made him look like a brute, but this impression was belied by his kind eyes and the warmth of his greeting for Brad. A brief handshake flowed into a hug. Brad barely managed to avoid spilling his beer on his former boss.

"It's good to see you," they said simultaneously.

Sarge smiled. "You're doing well for yourself. I always told you; you just needed more self-belief."

"That was certainly part of it. Some better thought processes helped too," Brad replied.

"Well, I could use some of that thinking on this case. 'Cos I can't believe who we think the perp is."

"Who?"

"We'll get to that. The tox report came back today and they identified the poison as belonging to a poison arrow frog or toad. Can you imagine?"

The idea was mind-boggling because his friend 'Froggy' had talked about them one time. He'd been an admirer of their bright colours, particularly *D. tinctorius azureus* – the blue poison dart frog. Such frogs weren't natives, nor could they be legally imported. But Brad imagined they could likely be smuggled in easily enough. Being cold-blooded and tiny they'd be hard to detect on a thermal scan and could easily be kept in a small container for a day's transport while they were brought into the country. Froggy had once compared them to the similarly colourful, Australian, corroboree frog, which produced its own toxin. This was unlike poison dart frogs whose got theirs from their diet. Froggy had then railed against the name corroboree frog as he felt it did an injustice to the Aboriginal ceremony which lent the frog its name. Though, he did acknowledge there was some evidence of Aboriginal men painting themselves like the frog for their ceremonies.

Brad frowned. "No. That's unbelievable." He knew with Sarge on the case, it could only lead to trouble for his friend. "And you have a suspect?"

"What was the phrase from one of the big city cases? We have a prime and only suspect."

"Froggy?" Brad asked, hoping he was wrong.

"Froggy," Sarge confirmed.

Brad picked up his beer and tried to look casual. "Have you charged him?"

"No, he's just in custody. We're making inquiries and are aiming to charge him over the weekend."

"So, you're saying if I want to help him, I've got to do it before I return to the city. That doesn't give me much time."

"About a day and half I reckon."

"Ooh, a ticking clock. I like it." He put down his beer without taking a sip. "Can I talk to him?"

"Not tonight. Maybe around mid-morning tomorrow?"

Brad nodded. "What motive are you thinking?"

"The case is pretty good. I'm mean he even wrote a paper" – Sarge pulled a paper out of his pocket and read off it – " about the blue poison dart frog being bred at Paignton Zoo in the UK. He'd even flown over and been part of the program. As for motive, well, I don't know how much you've followed some of the problems the town's been having due to the economic downturn, but let's just say the council's revenues are down as people aren't able to pay their rates, and the usual fundraisers aren't as successful as they used to be. What the farms produce just isn't being bought in the quantities it used to. The council is out of money, so they cut the grant for him to conserve local frog species. Mayor Jim led the call to cut the funding. To make it worse, Jim also advised Curtin Uni about their decision and they, in turn, reviewed Froggy's progress relating to his postgrad studies and suspended his … err stip-end. Is that how you say it?"

Brad shrugged. "So, the Mayor basically caused him to lose everything."

"Yes."

"Hmmm."

"What?"

"While I still don't think Froggy would do something like that, if it is him, I'm surprised the motivation wasn't to do with a jilted lover or partner of one of the Mayor's girlfriends."

"If it was one of them, my money's on Casey."

"Why does everyone think it's her? My sister said the same thing."

"You've met her, dated her even."

"Yes."

Sarge grinned. "So, you know then."

"I guess so. Still, what motive would she have?"

"She dated Froggy. No one's allowed to wrong a man of hers, past or present."

"True. It's why I stayed with her even when she treated me like sh— poorly at the end of the relationship, though I think by that time she was ready to move on and was trying to get rid of me. By having me end it, I guess she thought it would be better for me in the long run."

"Yeah, I can imagine how that might work."

Brad nodded, mentally working through what he knew, looking for a weakness in the case against his friend. It wasn't looking good.

"What's his explanation for the poison?"

"Doesn't have one. He said his frogs don't produce the toxin which killed the mayor."

"You'd told him which one it was, or did he slip and give himself away?"

Sarge paused. "No, I'd definitely told him what it was."

"I gotta go," Brad said after a pause. He felt a sudden urge to *feel* the town again by driving around it. Sarge nodded and pointed to Brad's drink.

"You can have it," Brad replied absently as he headed for the door.

Brad drove around the town, wishing he could be doing it on Froggy's motorcycle, which was a sporty Italian bike Brad was enamoured with. Northam wasn't known as the first motorcycle friendly town in the country for nothing. He drove past his old haunts and along the river, hoping for some inspiration. It was a shame to see several shops on the main street with for lease signs. He couldn't remember ever seeing that happen as a kid.

Two hours later he crept into his and Amy's bed and lay there for hours churning things over. His stomach turned. Was that due to missing his dinner? Or was it the fact the case against his friend looked disastrous, in that it seemed pretty strong?

Poor Froggy. What had happened to him? He'd been one of those rare kids who, even as a teenager, had embraced his quirks and relished being known as the guy who was obsessed with frogs and toads. He'd even encouraged the use of his nickname. What could have turned the loyal, funny guy he knew into a killer? Casey? Enough time with her could perhaps do it.

Brad drove the car to Johno's garage early the next morning. Both Johno and Emily were there. Brad shook Johno's hand. "Sorry about not catching you last night. We were pretty knackered after the week we've had. I wouldn't have been great company anyway. It turns out the main suspect is an old friend of mine."

"Yeah, I heard about Froggy. We all have."

Brad smiled wryly. "No secrets in this town."

"It's okay we didn't get to catch up. We can do that tonight when we have dinner with the outlaws."

Brad smiled politely. He wasn't a fan of that particular joke Johno used to refer to his parents-in-law: Brad's parents.

"True. I hope I can still make it. I can't believe they've arrested Froggy. No way he'd be capable of that kind of thing."

"Not when you knew him perhaps. But he's gotten darker in the last year or so. But still, I agree he wouldn't do something so extreme."

The way Johno used past tense to refer to Brad's relationship with Froggy stung. Had he really left the town behind to that extent?

"I'll do what I can for him," Brad said with conviction.

Brad's was the second car to arrive in the shop. Petey's ute was already there and ready to be raised by the hoist for an underbody inspection. Brad noticed a few patches of rust on the tray.

"So how long will it take?" Brad asked.

"We're just doing an oil change, lube and check-over of Petey's; that'll take an hour or so. Then it's on to yours, so I guess about midday. What're you gonna do now?" Johno asked.

"Go see Froggy and visit some old haunts. I might call into the pet shop in case they can tell me who they've sold a terrarium to in the last few months. Whoever did it would have needed to house the frog."

"Good idea," Emily replied.

Brad borrowed Emily's car and drove to the police station. He was soon in an interview room with his old friend, Froggy. It was hard to believe it was him. Brad's friend was dishevelled, which perhaps wasn't unexpected, but it was his demeanour which shocked Brad the most. He wouldn't hold eye contact, was twitchy and nowhere near the ebullient life-of-the-party character he'd grown up with. At least he seemed pleased to see Brad.

"You'll help me, won't you?" Froggy asked after they'd said hello.

"I'll do my best. But before that, what's happened to you? This," Brad gestured towards Froggy, "didn't just happen overnight. I mean, I've seen you after a night in the slammer before. This ain't that."

"I dated Casey."

"Not usually the wisest move."

"You know the hold she can have over you. She wore me down until I started dating her, then she became the most amazing girlfriend."

"Yep. Sounds like her."

"Then it went downhill and like that" – Froggy clicked his fingers – "it was all over. I'd been living with her, so found myself suddenly homeless. I managed to get a studio apartment on Main Street. It's super dingy, but that suited my mood. You know how she leaves you."

Brad nodded.

"How did you get over her?" Froggy asked, in a tone which suggested he still was not.

"I noticed when I was with her that women hated her, but not most of the men she'd dated once it had been a few months since they'd split. I think women could see she was just using her boyfriends. And I realised it wasn't anything I did. I think, despite our intimacy, she never really loved me. I was a project. Once she'd helped me come out of my shell a bit and start to show some drive she moved on. It wasn't me. It wasn't her. We just weren't an item anymore. Somehow that flicked a switch and instead of focusing on missing her and being angry at how she'd made us end, I focused on the good times we'd had. She only made me end it to make it easier to get over her."

Froggy looked at Brad with a strange expression which Brad struggled to read. Was it admiration? Jealousy? Relief at being given a means of getting over his loss?

"Fuck me, you've realised your potential," Froggy said with a grin. For a moment it was like old times. "You never would have stated it so well before."

Brad smiled, glanced upward and then grinned again.

"And the fact you've just appreciated the double meaning of 'realised' proves the point," Froggy said.

"She made me believe I could be a detective in the city. I'm grateful for that. It's been the making of me. So, I can't hate her that much. But enough about me. How can I help you?"

"Find the real poisoner."

"It's not you?"

"*No.*"

"Good. I had to ask. I'm only here unofficially, so I

don't have the power of the badge to compel information, but I'll try."

"Thanks. At least you'll start from the opinion I'm innocent. That helps."

"I was thinking of starting with the pet shop. Maybe they've sold some terrariums recently and can give me someone else to talk to."

Froggy shook his head. "They're not terrariums, they're vivariums. They have an aquatic and land-based section."

"Okay, vivarium then. But that's my only lead at the moment. I feel like I don't have enough data to point to anyone else. But I'll try find some."

"Make sure Sarge follows through on testing all my frogs. They don't produce the toxin which killed Jimmy. I think someone's trying to set me up since I've studied the frogs that do."

"That's good. Anything else?"

"Do you know the traditional way they extracted the toxin from the frogs for their darts? They trapped the frog in a hollow branch and poked it with sticks until it sweated the toxin, which they then collected – it's a thick viscous fluid – and then dipped their arrows in it. Maybe look for such a tube?"

"I'll keep it in mind. And trust me. I'll do what I can to get you released."

~

Northam was a town well-known for its farming community. Animals and pets were a way of life. As such, the town had two large pet stores. Both turned out to be unhelpful to Brad's investigation. The first didn't sell vivariums, and the second had only sold a very large enclosure for Petey's python. Brad knew Petey had owned his serpentine pet for years, and the sales assistant hadn't noticed any change in his other usual purchases of food and supplies. Brad still made a note to ask Petey about it. Once he'd completed his errands, he drove back to the garage to pick up his car.

"Any problems?" he asked Emily.

"Can you swap it for your squad car? You're not driving it enough. You're the exact opposite of Petey," Emily replied.

~

That night, with Amy, Emily and Johno, Brad had dinner with his parents. Brad was worried his parents might badger his sister now she was an underachiever, at least in their eyes. Since she'd returned to the town after losing her job, Emily had to put up with a constant stream of either, 'when are you going to get another real job' or 'why aren't you taking this opportunity to create some grandkids?' It had caused several arguments. At least the mayor's death could provide alternative conversation.

Once dinner was served Brad's father was quick to say he'd seen an article in the paper mentioning Brad in conjunction with a major drug bust.

"They're not meant to print my name, you know," Brad replied, downplaying the success. He knew how quickly this would turn into a jab at his sister. He'd put up with the reverse throughout his adolescence. It had strained his

86

relationship with his parents for years.

"I'd rather talk about what happened to the mayor," Amy interjected, winking at Brad.

It seemed everyone had an opinion on the case. Brad's mum thought Froggy had done it. "He was always so odd, playing with frogs," she said judgementally.

Emily repeated her assertion Casey was behind it, which sparked a conversation in which Brad was the only one to defend her. He was glad he and Amy had spoken about his prior relationship, so at least she was able to provide some support for Brad with the occasional, "that's not how Brad remembers it." Even Johno had a go at Brad for dating Casey. The argument started to get heated, so Brad decided to launch the nuclear option of changing the conversation.

"Guys, guys. Listen. I'm at a loss how to help Froggy, and he isn't even why Amy and I came down this weekend. Besides getting the car serviced, we're here to, um, share some news."

The rest of the conversation at the table duly went quiet in anticipation.

"The more observant of you may have noticed that despite Amy asking for a glass of wine, it's me who drank it."

"That's because I'm pregnant," Amy finished.

"That's why you warned her about Tammy jumping up!" Emily said. "I thought that was odd."

"Congratulations!" Brad's mum said, beaming. "How far along are you?"

"Eleven and a half weeks."

"Do you know if it's a boy or girl?" Brad's dad asked.

"Oh, Simon, it doesn't matter. We're finally going to be grandparents!" Brad's mum exclaimed while looking pointedly at Emily, who coughed in reply.

"Congratulations," Johno and Emily said simultaneously.

"Yeah, so some big changes ahead. We'll be converting the spare room to a nursery, so in a few months we won't have a spare room for you to stay in, but there's always spare apartments in the complex you can Airbnb," Brad said.

"We're not telling people just yet. I know we're pretty much at the second trimester, but it hasn't been the smoothest run so far, with some breakthrough bleeding, though it seems to have settled over the last fortnight. Anyway, we're holding off telling everyone else for a few more weeks," Amy said.

Eye contact from Brad to each other person, in turn, produced the response he was seeking of nods of understanding and some grunts of we won't tell. Brad wasn't sure he believed his mother.

~

Early on Sunday morning, Brad took Tammy for a walk to think through the case. All he kept picturing was Froggy's face imploring him for help. It hurt to be letting his friend down by making no progress. He was surprised to get a call from Samantha at 7.31 am. "Where are you?" she asked.

"What?"

"I'm at the lake for our fortnightly run."

Brad groaned. He'd forgotten about his regular social catch-up with the medical examiner.

"Oh, shit. Sorry. I'm at home for the weekend."

"Yeah, so you're a few minutes away?"

"Sorry, I mean I've gone back to Northam for the weekend. The car needed a service."

"Sure, that's logical. Your car needed a service so you decided to drive it a hundred kays for that. There's no other reason to go there. Nothing to tell anyone?"

"I don't know what you think you know, but anyway there's a second reason. There was a murder up here, and I'm trying to help my old Sergeant, and, as it turns out, an old friend."

"What happened?"

"The mayor was poisoned."

"Cool. What poison?"

"Not cool. But you'll like the poison. It was tetrodotoxin from a poison dart frog!"

"Wow, that is amazing. How'd they identify it was from a frog?"

"Huh?"

"Well, those frogs accumulate it from their diet. Plenty of marine animals do the same thing. It's not exclusive to frogs. That's why I'm curious."

"What other animals?" Could that be a clue? At least it would point away from Froggy.

"Several pufferfish, angelfish and *xanthid* crabs. It's the poison found in improperly prepared dishes of *fugu*, but the main source in this country would be the blue-ringed octopus, octopi, octopuses, whatever they're called."

"Really?"

"Yeah, but their dangerousness is greatly exaggerated. I mean every school kid is taught about them, but only three deaths have occurred in the last century from their bites."

"Hmm."

"What?"

"Dunno. Kinda wondering if maybe, just maybe, Mayor Jimmy didn't catch and eat one by mistake, or a crab or something. He did like fishing."

"Well, each blue-ringed octopus contains enough toxin to kill up to twenty-six adults. Cooking doesn't make a huge difference to the toxicity. So, it's possible he simply made a mistake and ate one. He'd be dead pretty quickly though. From memory, it's about half an hour before a lethal dose kills you. Their bites are tiny and often painless, so make sure the body is closely examined. It mightn't be obvious. The distinction between a bite and consumption could be important for you."

"Absolutely. The body was examined by a coroner though, not Steve, um, I think it was Cammy."

"I'll call you back. Gimme a minute."

Brad made Tammy sit, then knelt and scratched behind her ears. "This is exciting isn't it, girl? We might have a clue to get your uncle's friend out of jail!" Tammy licked his wrist in response. A moment later his phone rang.

"Okay, I have some info for you. Cammy dismissed

blue-rings due to the location of the victim, who couldn't have travelled that far from the ocean before dying. There was a scratch on his left arm. Nothing in the stomach though, other than some beer and a sausage and bread he'd been witnessed eating at a shire event that afternoon. It'd be pretty hard to target him from a sausage sizzle."

"Agreed. Would there be any distinguishing feature to an octopus bite?"

"Not really. It'll look like any other puncture wound. If the bite victim doesn't die quickly, then you'll get a secondary circle of infection, but there wasn't one on the body."

"It's an alkaloid, yeah?"

"Yep. You've been reading."

"I couldn't sleep, so I read about it on my phone; it's how I knew how to pronounce tetrodotoxin. Alkaloids are really bitter. You said there was beer in the stomach. Was it a VB?"

Like most West Australian's Brad refused to say the full name of the beer. No one from his town acknowledged good things could come from 'over east'.

"I don't know if they ID'd the particular beer, but I see where you're going. You think they concealed the poison in the beer."

"Makes sense."

"That was Cammy's conclusion too. Damn, dude, you're getting good at this."

"Thanks. Unfortunately, that doesn't help my mate. The setup is too good. What's more Northam than burying the hatchet, so-to-speak, over a beer? I just can't believe Froggy would do something like that."

"Hold up, your mate's name is Froggy?"

"It's a nickname. He studies, err, studied frogs."

"Well, if it was a blue-ring, you've at least got some grounds to look for alternative suspects."

"And I've only got a few hours left to do it. I'm heading back this afternoon and this isn't my case. I'm just helping out."

Sam laughed. "So, you're a consulting detective! Where have I heard that before?"

"Thanks for always seeing the humour, Sam."

"Yeah, well, on a serious note, it's not a good way to go. It starts with a pins and needles sensation of the lips and tongue as they start to numb, and is soon followed by tremors, nausea and strong abdominal pain. Your vic seems to have had such a large dose he didn't even vomit or get diarrhoea before he died. The person slowly loses the ability to breathe as paralysis sets in. They're fully conscious as they lose control over their body. Just imagine every brain cell firing, trying to tell your damned body to breathe, but all you get in response is a sense of suffocation. Cammy corrected me and said death usually takes four to six hours. Your guy was seen feeling okay twenty minutes before he died. From then he must have fallen ill, and for most of the time that followed he probably couldn't move or speak. It must have been a very large dose. He couldn't do anything to help his situation. That's a good ten minutes of knowing you're about to die.

To me that's terrifying. I can't think of many worse ways to go."

Brad shuddered. "Why do I suddenly feel like I'm losing the ability to breathe?"

"Mirror neurons. You have them in spades. It's why you're such an empathetic guy. Amy's lucky to have a husband like that. It's also why you'll make a good dad someday."

Brad inhaled sharply. Did she know? "Thanks," he said.

"Why are the good ones always taken?"

"Because we're the good ones. Oh, and by the way you were right."

Brad disconnected the call and smiled. That last statement would give her something to think about. Brad mentally smacked his head when he realised he still hadn't asked her why she was at the station a few days before.

~

After the call, Brad marvelled at the thought a blue-ringed octopus could be behind a death in outback Western Australia. It reminded him of the famous urban legend of the body of a scuba diver found in a tree in the forest. According to the legend, it was concluded a water bomber had scooped up the hapless diver while firefighting and dropped him on the tree. Could something similar have occurred here? Brad thought it unlikely. Firefighters wouldn't use seawater here; the ocean was just too far away, especially as the Avon and Mortlock Rivers were so convenient. Besides, Northam had escaped the recent large-scale fires which had plagued the country over the summer.

Was the information that there were other ways of getting the toxin the extra data Brad needed? His heart thumped at the thought. Shifting the source of the poison helped Froggy, but didn't put him in the clear. Brad put himself in the shoes of a criminal. Let's say he wanted to use blue-ring tetrodotoxin to kill someone. How would he get it? He'd catch a blue-ring and take it home. He'd learn how to milk the poison, extract it, and then use it. That might take some time and practice. How would he care for the octopus? He'd have to make sure it had the right water, but he wouldn't want it to be traced by buying supplies through a pet shop. Would he test the poison first? Probably, but not on a human. Maybe an animal? He'd want to spread the tests out to avoid raising an alarm.

Brad did a quick search for the local veterinary clinic, and luckily it was open twenty-four hours a day. Brad ran Tammy back to his sisters, and jumped into his car. A short drive later, he walked through their manual opening doors and into a waiting room. The sound of a dog whimpering emanated from a treatment room. The thought of a dog in pain made Brad wince. He approached the vet nurse/receptionist who was typing something into a computer. She was sitting in a swivel chair facing away from the counter. There was something familiar about her shape. Upon the counter was a cookie – Casey's favourite snack. As she swivelled around at the sound of his footfall, Brad knew why. It *was* Casey.

Brad was momentarily speechless. He wasn't expecting

to see her.

"Uh, um, hi, Casey, uh…"

"Oh, hi, other Sarge. I heard you were in town. I hope you're not visiting to ask me out. I've sworn off married men." Brad felt his brain go on pause, and his face freeze. She was so, so … nope, he couldn't think of a suitable word. Brad forced himself to picture Amy and their joy when the two lines appeared on the pregnancy test after months of trying. The thought was sufficient to give Brad some grounding.

"Uh, no. I was just coming in to see if, in the last few months, there have been any pets that have died, but were unusually floppy when brought in?"

"Yeah, sure. There was Benny's dog about a month ago. Floppy as a wet towel. Must've been bitten or eaten something he shouldn't."

"Any others?"

As Casey scratched her head, Brad was reminded how she could turn a simple act into something sexual. In this case it was her deep inhalation as she did so. It raised her chest and the movement caught Brad's eye.

"Now you mention it, one of Jimmy's sheep was found like that. They incinerated it."

"Any idea what caused it?"

"Nah. We don't usually do autopsies unless there's a spate of deaths or the owner requests it. It's not cost-effective."

"Thanks."

"Sure. Anything else?"

Brad bit his cheek but then decided to ask his question anyway. "You seeing anyone?"

"I had a few dates with the mayor on the q.t. But I guess that's over, so not at the moment."

Her nonchalance at her boyfriend's passing reminded Brad why she was not a suitable partner. She just didn't form that kind of long-term attachment. Could it also mean she had something to do with it?

"Thanks again," Brad said absently, as he turned and left. He only just registered Casey saying, "Anytime, Sarge."

~

Brad returned to his car. At least he had an indication he was on the right track. Brad knew how sensitive fish were to environmental changes from the pet fish his parents had while he was growing up. He assumed the same was true for invertebrates. So, you'd want to replenish with water from where you found the octopus. That could involve a few trips.

Brad googled places you could find a blue-ringed octopus. One of the first articles was about one found around a year ago in Geraldton. At nearly a thousand-kilometre round trip, that would be quite the drive to do repeatedly. It would take a weekend each time. Not to mention the wear and tear on the car.

With a start, Brad realised why Petey's ute was being serviced so often. The usual rush of the killer identifying epiphany was raised further by the relief he could be about to free his old friend. His heart thumping, Brad looked to the sky and exhaled forcefully. He could help Froggy after all.

Brad called Sarge and ten minutes later they were knocking on Petey's door. Without a warrant, they couldn't compel him to let them search his house, but the culture of the town was such that if Sarge asked you to do something to help keep the peace, you did it. It would be more incriminating for him to say no.

Petey answered the door, dressed in nothing but a bathrobe. Brad was relieved it was tied.

"Hey, Bradee, long time. Hi, Sarge. What's up?"

"We'd like to talk to you about the mayor's death," Sarge said.

Petey's eyes widened. "Why?" He sounded alarmed and looked guilty.

Brad's skin prickled. It seemed they'd found their killer.

"We know you've been driving to Geraldton to get seawater for a blue-ringed octopus."

It was a surprise when Petey's expression shifted from alarm to a broad grin. "Nah, man, that wasn't me. That was Froggy. He's been borrowing my ute to go visit some girl he met online up there. His bike's no good for that kind of trip."

Brad felt like the worn rug he was standing on had been pulled from under him. Froggy *was* the real killer. Froggy must have thought he was being clever using blue-ringed octopus venom, never expecting the venom would be mistaken as being of frog origin. It was a reasonable assumption. It was only that the coroner accounted for the victim being so far from the ocean which derailed the plan. It also explained why Froggy wanted his frogs tested. The results would show no link between him and the poison, even though his research had taught him all about it.

~

A quick apology and short car ride later, and Brad and Sarge were in the interview room with Froggy. As soon as he saw them, he read the mood.

"No luck helping me out?" he asked.

"Worse," Brad replied.

"Oh. Do I bother to ask what?"

"You shouldn't have asked me for help. I've only found more reasons to charge you."

"Which is what I'm going to do now. You're being formally charged with the murder of Mayor Jimmy Shireman," Sarge said.

Sarge told Froggy his rights. Froggy acknowledged he understood. Brad went through the steps Froggy had taken in the lead-up to killing the mayor:

"So, you obtained the blue-ringed octopus by driving to Geraldton, then kept going back to get replacement water for the tank you kept it in. You practised or tested the venom on at least a dog and a sheep that we know of, then waited for the right opportunity to get Jimmy. The fundraiser was perfect. There would be so many people around it'd be near impossible to attribute the poisoning to a specific attendee, and then you slipped the poison into his beer. Was that at the sausage sizzle, or did you go to his home?"

Froggy slumped further and further into his chair as Brad spoke. He raised his head. "At the BBQ. I expected him to collapse in the crowd. I didn't realise he'd go home the moment he started feeling unwell."

"How'd you find the octopus?" Sarge asked.

"I found an article they'd been seen in Geraldton, so I borrowed Petey's ute, as I couldn't carry the right gear on the bike, made up a story about seeing a girl, and off I went. The usually well-camouflaged octopi were easy for me to spot due to all my practise finding frogs. Once you know what to look for it's easier. Other than that, you seem to know the rest."

"There's one big thing though. Why? The mate I knew not only wouldn't do this, but couldn't," Brad said.

"Things have changed over the years since you left. My research hasn't been going well, and I haven't done anything of note academically since the breeding at Paignton Zoo. I'd been given a warning by the uni to publish something soon. That was right when Casey broke up with me. She'd treated me horribly for a while and told me the reason I couldn't publish anything was because I wasn't a good enough man, but I couldn't leave her. I think I'm the first man who actually got her to say she was leaving, not the other way round. Then I saw Jimmy on a date with her. I knew I'd never be able to resume our relationship. That hurt and I blamed Jimmy. When he cut my funding and then my research grant from the uni … you've got to understand he ruined my life. Casey wouldn't stand for it if the situation applied to her. I wanted to be the man she wanted me to be, so I started plotting how to stand up for myself. I concluded Jimmy needed to be out of the picture. I mean how many marriages has he broken up? Three? Four? How many relationships? Even more. I was doing the town a favour."

Brad sighed. "It hurts to see you so misguided. Casey wouldn't want you to take the coward's way of murder. She'd want you to challenge Jimmy for the mayorship. That's how you could win her respect, restore some of your funding and get some of your self-respect back."

Froggy groaned. "I'm an idiot. How can you be here for all of five minutes and see that, when I couldn't in months?"

"You're not an idiot. Just lacking a mate to talk things through. I'm sorry I haven't kept in better contact. I could have helped you."

"You think this is your fault?"

"No. But I could have helped you through your rough patch. I will come to visit you in jail." Brad said the last sentence with conviction. "I'll also arrange for you to get access to resources which helped me improve my thinking. With good behaviour, you'll be out in decade or so. You can come out a new man, or someone more broken than you already are. You're young enough that by the time you're out, you'll have half your life still to live. Don't throw that away by becoming bitter."

A tear rolled down Froggy's cheek.

"Thanks, Bradee."

"You're still my friend," Brad said softly.

Froggy started crying more openly. "You can't get me out of this?"

"No." Brad shook his head for emphasis. It was out of his control. Besides, Froggy had committed *murder*. That couldn't be brushed off. "But I will be a character witness if you want, even though that might cause problems for me – being seen defending a killer, I mean."

"Thanks."

"From what some of one of my informant's friends have told me, it's important to remember the outside while you're in jail. Don't think of it as being all there is. That's why I'm saying I'll visit you and help you reinvent yourself while you're in there. Don't let it become a death sentence for you."

Sarge stood and placed a hand on Froggy. He nodded to Brad and then the door. Brad stood and repeated Sarge's action on Froggy.

"I'll visit too," Sarge said.

Froggy crumbled into the table, sobbing. Brad and Sarge left the room. In the hallway, Sarge stopped Brad. "You're a good man, Brad. What you did in there, that was" – Sarge patted Brad on the back and thanked him for his help.

"Always ready to lend a hand whenever you need me, Sarge."

~

That afternoon, as Amy and Brad drove back to the city, Samantha called in response to a text from Brad asking her to call.

"Greetings, Sam. We're both here."

"Hi, Amy," Samantha said enthusiastically.

"Hi, Sam," Amy replied.

"Thanks for the chat this morning. Instead of helping me free my friend, it enabled me to make the case against him many times stronger," Brad said.

"Shit. Shame it was him. That must've sucked."

"Yeah. But at least the right person is going to jail."

"So, uh, anything you guys want to tell me?"

"Yes, but first, why were you at the station the other day? It's been bugging me I didn't ask."

"Oh that. A lady never tells."

"Yeah, but you know the response I'd make to that."

"Hey, I am a lady. Anyhoo, I was there to see Detective Summers. She had an interesting case of someone bleeding to death. I had some interesting pathology for her and needed to get out of the office for a bit. Sometimes it's all a bit much and it's good to get among the living, especially those who are trying to make the world a better place. The vic's brachial artery was slashed in a unique way."

Brad nodded.

"Even though I'm driving, I can tell you Brad's nodding his head in satisfaction of that explanation," Amy said. "So, in response to your question. Yes, we do have news, but you have to keep it to yourself. Though it seems you've already divined it." Amy motioned one, two, three, with the fingers of her left hand while the palm was still on the wheel.

"We're pregnant."

"Yay. Congrats, guys. I'd guessed as much, but to hear it is so cool. Can't wait to spoil the little kid rotten as his not-real-aunt-but-still-aunty."

"We'll hold you to that," Brad said.

"Awesome." Sam paused for a few beats, then laughed. "Lemme guess, Brad is already wondering about the pathology I gave Sally."

Brad smiled and noticed Amy glance at him.

"Yup," he and Amy said together. Brad made a note to check in with his detective the following day. After all, what was better than solving one case, than the satisfaction of moving on to the next?

Green
Fuller

It had been a great Easter break. Samantha had extended the holiday with a few days of annual leave and the extra time had produced a restful frame of mind. She had spent much of the time zoning out and trying to forget about her recent cases. Samantha had binge watched some shows on her laptop either in a hot bath or lying on her bed, but also managed a couple of decent runs around Lake Monger. For the most part though, she'd stayed home. The icing on the relax-a-cake was that the indie book she'd taken a punt on had turned out to be to her liking and well-written.

All these happy thoughts of her extra-long weekend dissipated as Samantha looked at the body of the teenager lying on her dissecting table. She hated doing autopsies on young people, and this case had all the hallmarks of a tragedy. The auburn haired, green-eyed girl should have been a popular student at her school; she was in the academically advanced class, captain of the netball team and sang in a school band. However, over the last several months she'd started keeping to herself, alienating her friends, and, according to the case report, appeared anxious.

The girl's name was Nigella, which Samantha knew was derived from a word meaning black. In contrast to her name Nigella's skin was a freckled porcelain white. She'd collapsed during a presentation to her class. She'd started the report on *Crime and Punishment* looking flushed and shaky. A classmate said she was radiating heat. Her report was described as confused and raspy, and ended with her vomiting before she fainted to the floor. Nigella had died on the way to hospital.

A sample of the vomit had been collected and, unusually, it appeared to contain soil. Samantha wondered if, perhaps, she might have her first case of pica. Pica was a psychological disorder characterised by an appetite for substances which are largely non-nutritive, such as ice, metal, soil or chalk. The issue she had was that pica wouldn't explain the cause of death as soil wasn't usually toxic.

Samantha cleared her mind, as she always did before an autopsy. It was better to start without a preconceived idea of what killed someone and let the pathology do the talking.

She began her examination of the naked body and was shocked to see a rose-coloured rash on the back of her waist. How had no one alerted her to it? With the other symptoms in the file, it was likely to be a form of enteric fever. She should be in a hazmat suit.

The body was returned to its refrigerated compartment,

while Samantha went to follow up on how the spots could have been missed. She went to her office, which she shared with her junior ME, Steve. Steve hung up the phone at his desk as she entered.

"Oh, perfect timing. That was Hannah from RPH. She said they inadvertently rushed sending the girl on your case load for today. It seems they were waiting on some blood and stool-work, which has just come in, and that's when they realised the body had already shipped. It's likely a case of typhoid."

"No shit. I'd started the examination and could tell that at a glance. How could they be so stupid?"

"Calm down. I'm sure it was just a post-holiday slip."

"I might've been infected."

"Did you eat the same food or kiss her?"

"Of course not."

"Then you're fine. I'm sure she's no Typhoid Mary. If you're worried get one of the attendings over at RPH to prescribe you some ciprofloxacin and drink an extra glass or two of water today."

"Ugh. I know you're right. Can you get back on the phone and give them a serve for me? At least I hadn't cut her yet."

Steve nodded and Samantha left to go back to the morgue.

~

Her hazmat suit produced mixed feelings. On the one hand she felt invulnerable to the world when in it, but on the other she also felt claustrophobic. As Samantha cleared her mind again, she wondered why such an obviously sick girl would still go to school and why she wouldn't seek help? It was unfathomable. To become fatal, the illness had to progress over days without intervention.

Why wouldn't she seek help or at least stay home? Samantha asked herself again as she began the y-shaped cut to start the autopsy.

Three hours later, she finished the procedure and returned the body to storage. It was a relief to take off the hazmat suit. Samantha went to her office and phoned her friend, Sergeant Brad Thomas. After discussing where they'd go for a run on the weekend, she got to the purpose of her call.

"I've just autopsied Nigella Mead and it's not good."

"Hang on. Who is that? I don't think she's one of my cases."

"She wasn't. She is now. Sorry. It's just too weird."

"Uh, okay."

"She turned eighteen a month ago. She collapsed yesterday in her first class back at school after the break. She was suffering from typhoid, which appears to have been contracted by eating soil. I found soil in her stomach and bowel."

"Why would she eat soil?"

"There's a psychological disorder called pica which could explain it. It's straightforward to diagnose. The person must have been eating non-nutritive non-foods for at least a month. The eating must be considered abnormal for the person's stage of development, so an infant eating sand in the sandpit wouldn't be a problem. The eating also needs to be considered not normal from a cultural point of view."

"Such as?"

"Off the top of my head there's an African tribe where the women eat clay during pregnancy to ward off cravings. Apparently it works well for them."

"Eww. Don't tell Amy that. Her cravings can be satisfied the old-fashioned way, by her demanding I get for her whatever she wants when she wants it."

Samantha laughed. "Any interesting ones so far?"

"The other day she had me put soy sauce in her hot chocolate. She drank it quite happily too. I couldn't look away while she was drinking it, so I copped a telling off for making her feel self-conscious."

"I can say that pregnancy wasn't the cause with Nigella. In fact, I'd guess she was a virgin."

"You can tell that?"

"Nope, not even a little bit. But, if your idea of eating out is grabbing a soil sandwich then you'd probably be limited in your choice of restaurant for a date."

"I guess so, but there are less—"

"I know, but there are no signs of trauma there."

"Can we move off this topic?"

"Sure, because here's the kicker. I don't think she died from typhoid, or at least not only typhoid. She had soil through her system, which indicates regular consumption. There was a shift in the make-up of the soil though. The stuff at the end of her bowel was more clay-like, and the stuff in her stomach and the vomit was sandy."

"Meaning?"

"Meaning, she'd likely eaten some on the spur of the moment near her school. The campus isn't too far from the Mindarie marina, and I'd guess the soil is sandy there."

"So, it was compulsive?"

"I'm not sure. I'd think so, but that wasn't all that was wrong with her."

"Pica, typhoid and something else? Let me guess … nope, can't think of a thing."

"She had ARDS."

"Can you translate that for me?"

"Acute Respiratory Distress Syndrome."

"So, her lungs weren't working?"

"Spot on. The X-rays showed it first. Normal lungs show as black on the photos; hers were like someone had smeared a small amount of white paint over the picture. That's bad. She'd have been dead in a few days from that alone, if it wasn't what killed her."

"But she went to school!"

"I know. I've sent more blood, stool and urine to the lab for screening. There's too much going on that doesn't add up, which is why I need you to do some investigation for me."

"What do you need?"

"Interview her friends at school, speak to her teachers, see if they can cast any light on the matter. Then how about we go to her home and search, search, search. I have no idea what to look for, but I need your eye to spot what

110

doesn't add up. You're good at that and between us we should find something if it's there."

"Thanks."

"Oh, and try find her diary. It's a hunch, but her strange behaviours mean she must have had a lot going through her mind. I'd think it's likely she would have written stuff. Poetry, stories or diary or whatnot. And not on PC, on paper."

"Why not on computer?"

"It's not the same," Samantha said forcefully.

"Uh, anything I should know?"

"My past is my past. I don't think that way anymore. One day when we can talk round a campfire with a few drinks, I'll tell you. You don't get into my line of work without some affinity for dark things."

"It'll be a while before campfire talks and drinks will happen. Amy's in no state to be up for camping, and it'll be a long time before I'd feel comfortable taking a baby out bush, but I'll hold you to that."

"Deal."

Samantha disconnected the call. Brad's astute comment on her remark at least convinced her she had the right detective for her task.

~

Brad started at Nigella's school. Her teachers were all in agreement. She was a popular and social girl in year 11, but in year 12 had inexplicably isolated herself. Her grades had improved though, and she was on track to be in the upper tier of the school's results in December. Two teachers identified Tiffany Thomason as a friend or former friend. Neither were particularly sure. Brad interviewed Tiffany next.

Tiffany confirmed they'd been close the previous year, but that Nigella had pushed her away at the start of their final year of high school.

"I saw her in the maintenance shed last week before the break. She was doing something weird."

"Go on," Brad encouraged.

"The maintenance guy, Terry" – Tiffany shuddered – "he's so icky. He made friends with a stray cat which comes on campus. He feeds it and it's kind of become an unofficial school mascot. Anyway, he even had a litter tray for it."

Brad found himself frowning at the odd detail. Why would she mention that? Tiffany leaned in conspiratorially.

"She was *eating the cat litter*." Tiffany nodded as if to confirm the veracity of her story.

"That is weird," Brad replied. He didn't want to let on they knew about such acts.

After their interview he visited the maintenance shed. Terry wasn't around which made it easy to get a small sample of the kitty litter. He wasn't sure what it could be used for, but it seemed like it should be tested, especially since it was the clay kind rather than paper.

~

After a coffee stop, Brad arrived at Nigella's house, having asked Samantha to meet him there. His intuition said he needed to search for any potential diary unhindered, but he couldn't say why. Samantha agreed to provide cover while he looked around. On their approach to the front door, Brad noticed a neighbour's curtain flutter. Were they watching the house? Nigella's stepmother, Arlene, let them in and consented to a search once they emphasised they were there due to the typhoid and to look for a source.

Samantha sat with Arlene and nodded to Brad to hunt for what she'd asked. Brad went straight to Nigella's bedroom.

If he was a teenage girl, where would he hide a diary? It wouldn't be under the mattress or in a pillow, as those were too obvious and clichéd. Under the floor? That was also a cliché. The room was carpeted, so it seemed unlikely. Brad carefully examined where the carpet met the walls of the room anyway, in case there was a section which could be pulled back. He didn't find one. If there were a diary, surely it would be in Nigella's bedroom. She'd want it to be accessible, but not in sight and not in a drawer or some easily searchable place. He searched the drawers anyway. None had any false bottoms or revealed anything of use.

Look for wear patterns, he told himself. It was a regular mantra for him. The desk was neat and a slight discolouration on the right side near the edge only revealed Nigella was probably left-handed and rested her opposite elbow there when studying.

The chair was wooden and not on casters like he'd expect a teenager's study chair to be. There were no obvious indentations in the carpet from the chair legs other than around the desk, so if there was a diary and it was in a hard-to-reach place, such a place would have to be reached by standing on the bed.

Brad looked around the room again. It'd have to be in the built-in wardrobe. He moved one of the two sliding doors to the side. Nigella's bed was close enough to the wardrobe that if she stood on her mattress, she could reach the upper shelf. Brad mimicked the action, but when he moved the suitcase on the shelf, he could feel from its weight that it was empty. He shook it side to side to be sure. Under the upper shelf was hanging space and shelves. A press on the clothes didn't reveal anything solid hidden in them. Brad was getting ready to give up. He sat on the bed and wondered what to do. There had to be something here to give Samantha and him more data. Without it, it would be hard to reach a conclusion in the case.

The wardrobe was still the most likely place. Brad stood on the bed again and ran his fingers over the top shelf. The task involved awkwardly twisting his arm due to the limited access from the shelf being blocked by the wall above the cupboard doors. The search, like resistance to the Borg, was futile. As he pushed himself back from leaning against the frame of the sliding doors, he noticed a slight smudge on the other side of the architrave. The sight gave him hope. He swapped the doors to the other side and shuffled along the edge of the bed. Running his hand along the interior where the wall met the door, his pulse raised when his hand hit what felt like a book-like bump on the wall. Gripping the object with his fingers and a giving a slight pull caused the distinct sound of Velcro tabs being ripped off their corresponding attachment.

Brad pulled his hand back to reveal an A5 sized, leather-bound journal. It was held closed by a built-in piece of elastic. The initials N.F.M. were embossed on the cover. Brad undid the elastic and flicked through. It was clear it was what they were after, but he'd already spent too long in the room. Arlene might start wondering what was taking him so long. Brad hid the diary amongst his kit and returned to the living room with a forlorn expression.

"Nothing there. Would you mind if I looked around outside?" Brad asked.

Arlene gave a wan smile. "Sure."

Brad went through the living room to the backyard. He was surprised to see that other than a shed, it contained only lawn. There were no plants and, to Brad's surprise, no weeds. The lawn was the most immaculate he'd ever seen. He took a sample of the soil, noting a faint odour of sewage. The lawn was so lush, he couldn't see where Nigella would have taken soil from for eating, though where it met the fence, a v-shaped drainage line had been dug. He noted one section appeared to have a more acute downward angle. Could Nigella have taken soil and smoothed it over to conceal the act?

The shed contained the usual gardening tools: a bike, lawnmower, and a variety of chemicals. There was motor oil, a light-green coolant, a bottle of blue glass cleaner and a dark-green weedkiller Brad recognised as the same one his parents used on their farm when he was growing up.

Brad returned to the living room and, standing behind

Arlene, nodded to Samantha. She took the hint and wrapped up her interview. "Thank you, Arlene, for helping us. I know this must be a difficult time for you. Your information on Nigella's habits will help us a lot."

Arlene nodded and dabbed her eyes. Brad hadn't noticed any tears. Was she acting?

"Was there anything I need to see?" Samantha asked Brad.

"No. There is some soil in the back which might be contaminated by sewage, but that was all I could find."

"Oh that. That's blood and bone, not sewage," Arlene said.

"Okay," Brad replied.

"My associate," Samantha gestured to Brad, "has taken some samples for me to analyse." Brad held up his armful of bags. "We don't think you're at risk, but obviously, that is our primary concern. We do need to find out where the bacteria came from though, so if anything occurs to you, could you please give us a call?" Samantha handed over her business card.

~

On the way to their cars, keeping his back to the house, Brad gave Samantha the samples he'd collected.

"I don't know if these are of any use. Nigella was seen eating kitty litter by her friend, and the soil is from the backyard. I also found her diary. I didn't get much chance to look at it, but I did see something about her ordering earth online. Does that make sense?"

"Wait, she was ordering the dirt? How? There's

something else going on here. Pica cases tend to be more compulsive than that. Would you mind if I took the diary? I think I might be able to spot if there's something useful pathology-wise better than you."

"Fair enough, but follow normal chain of custody rules so it's admissible if needed. You're in a better place to work out if there's anything in there which may indicate why she died. Though, from what I can see, it's a case of accidental self-harm. That's not illegal."

"That's the thing. Some of her symptoms could be caused by poisoning, but with her strange eating, it'd be hard to prove she hadn't consumed something she shouldn't."

"Maybe that's why she didn't seek medical treatment? She was afraid they'd stop her eating dirt."

"It's definitely possible. This is what sucks about hard to determine causes of death. You can't just ask them like you can a witness."

"Did you get anything from Arlene?"

"Only that Nigella liked to party and would drink anything given to her."

"What about Arlene herself?"

"She used to be an engineer, but had to quit after her thumb was ripped off in an accident at work. It took a chunk of her palm too. It was from her dominant left hand and it took so long to recover, plus the scarring from the incident itself; she couldn't go back to that workplace. Then her husband died. Everything came undone. Her share of the inheritance meant she didn't need to return to work for a few years and by the time she was ready the mining boom had turned to bust, and the downturn hit."

"That must have been hard for her."

"It was. She seemed very bitter about the whole thing."

The neighbour Brad had spotted spying on them came out of his house. He pointed to Brad, his car and a point further down the street. A tilt of his head confirmed his desire. Brad was to make it seem like he was leaving, drive a few hundred metres down the street and talk to him there. Brad wondered why the neighbour didn't seem to want to talk to Samantha as well. Samantha saw the gesture and turned to Brad. "You go. I'll head back to the office and start the analyses of the dirt and diary."

~

"Thanks for talking to me." The elderly gentleman Brad was talking to seemed kind-hearted enough, but he spoke only just above a whisper and leant forward like he was taking part in a conspiracy. "Are you a cop?"

Brad's business shirt and pants meant it wasn't a given. His ID was in his pocket. He decided to go with the truth. "Yes."

"Good. Nigella was a friend of mine. I used to play the piano for her while she sang, and what a voice she had, but after Christmas, something happened and she stopped our weekly sessions. Then, in late February, I think, she asked if she could get some online purchases delivered to me instead of her home. Something about not wanting her mother to know what she was buying." The man sneered. "You know how women are."

Brad tried to conceal a scowl. While the man may not have been an out and out bigot, he still clearly thought women were secretive and mysterious. That was ignorant.

"Do you know what it was?" Brad asked.

"That's the thing. It wasn't anything particularly odd, just some cosmetics. A delivery came for her today. Here." He handed over a package from a well-known online retailer. "It was meant to arrive last week. She hasn't called in to see if it'd arrived. What's happened to her?"

Brad was surprised the man didn't know. He'd assumed he was trying to find out what the police knew.

"She, uh, passed away yesterday."

The old man fell silent and appeared crestfallen. His eyes welled with tears. "She was a good kid. She never said much about what killed the spark in her this year, but I'd bet my savings it was something to do with her mother."

"Her mother?"

"Well, stepmother, but she practically raised Nigella after her dad died six years ago. He was a good man. I knew him too. He had a heart attack. It took long enough that he realised what was happening, sought Nigella and made her promise to make something of herself before he passed."

So that's what was driving her. It was, at least, a possible explanation for why she wouldn't miss school, despite being ill.

"I think you're the first adults who've visited the house since the month after her dad died. That's how I knew I had to talk to you."

Brad extracted two cards from his wallet. "Here are my contact details. Can you write yours on this second card?"

The man did so, using Brad's pen, then turned and began a slow, slumped walk back to his house. Brad called Samantha and filled her in on the talk.

~

When Samantha arrived back at her office she was annoyed the additional bloodwork she'd ordered on Nigella hadn't come through. She sent down the soil samples with a note to bring them or the bloodwork up the moment they were done.

Samantha made herself a mug of tea and sat down to read the diary. The first entry was from about a year before, and the first few months were run of the mill teenage girl thoughts. Nigella had a crush on a boy named Arjun. She was nervous about singing in front of the school in an assembly. Her friend Tiffany had gone all the way with a boy, and that made Nigella wonder what it would be like. It seemed she was a reasonably popular kid who was a bit of a socialite. Everything changed after New Year's Eve. The year began with Nigella being excited about turning eighteen in a few months and finally becoming an adult. Her trust fund would convert to her very own bank account, and she was looking forward to buying a car. Her friends would be so jealous when she was able to drive herself to school. Then there was an entry dated January 7th.

> *I cracked Mum's phone today. Her password was 270302, the day before I was born. It's like she thinks that was her*

*last day of freedom or something. It got worse though. Her social media was full of posts about me wanting to get drunk or high, and being caught doing a shot of vanilla essence, and later methylated spirits. The posts were all fake. **I'd never do that.** Most posts were variations of how Mum was dreading what I'd get up to once I turn eighteen.*

The next few days entries were variations of confusion about why her mum would want to say such things about her daughter:

I figured it out. Mum wants my inheritance and to be rid of me. I knew she never loved me, but I never thought she'd go this far. I think she's going to kill me. Her posts about me drinking random things make me think she wants to poison me. If I die once I'm eighteen she'll get my trust fund. If I die before then it goes to my cousin, so I'm safe for a few months.

And a week later:

I've searched the whole house. I think she's planning on using paraquat. There's a brand new bottle in the shed. It's the only new thing she's bought for a while. Her socials are setting me up so if I die from it, she'll have evidence I was recklessly drinking things to get high.

Samantha recoiled. How could someone do that to a anyone, let alone a child they raised? Paraquat was a dark green liquid, and was one of the most widely used herbicides. It killed green plant tissue on contact and was toxic to humans. It had been linked to the development of Parkinson's disease and was banned in several countries, but not Australia. Samantha's head spun as she remembered ingestion of it could lead to acute respiratory distress syndrome. She read on. The next pertinent entry was from the end of January:

> *I'm going to be the best student this year. Mum will have a hard time selling her story.*

Valentine's Day didn't have anything to do with love:

> *I've bought a prepaid credit card. Mr Almeida from next door will let me order stuff to his house. I'm going to buy Fuller's earth. I'll tell him it's for homemade make-up. Much better than buying kitty litter for a cat I don't have.*

Samantha dropped the diary to her desk. The poor girl. She didn't have pica. Samantha called Brad.

"I'm not sure where you are, but you probably should go and arrest Nigella's mother." Samantha could feel, as much as hear, the bitter tone in her voice.

"I thought she died because she ate contaminated soil."

"She didn't have pica."

"So, what killed her?"

"Her diary gives the story. She'd worked out her mother wanted her dead and would likely poison her with paraquat."

"I saw a bottle of that in their shed. I grew up in a farming community. We used to use it all the time. I just assumed that was why her lawn was so lush. Any weeds were obliterated by it."

"The poison is deadly for humans. Don't you remember the paraquat murders?"

"Huh?"

"They were a series of poisonings in Japan in 1985."

Brad laughed. "I wasn't born until the following year,

122

so no, I don't remember them."

"I was a year old. But we were taught about them when I was in year 10 as part of a forensics elective. Police were unable to gather any evidence about the murders other than they were caused by a poisoned beverage that was left inside or around vending machines. Unsuspecting victims would think they'd scored a free drink and die when they drank it. There were twelve murders between April and November. After vending machine operators posted warnings on machines the poisonings stopped. But they never found the culprit."

"And the relevance?"

"Maybe that's where Arlene got the idea? She must be about fifty. She'd have been old enough to take notice when those murders happened. Plus, it suggests it can be hidden in food."

Brad nodded. "Good thinking."

"Here's the thing about the poison. There are no specific antidotes, but Fuller's earth is an effective treatment if taken in time. She was eating it as a medicinal clay! The same compound was in clay kitty litter, which explained her eating that too. She must've been worried because she was feeling sick and thought it would help. She'd run out of Fuller's and her next delivery was delayed due to the long weekend. She was desperate. She felt she needed something, anything, to counteract another dose. She wasn't to know this time she was sick due to typhoid rather than paraquat."

"There was a faint scent of sewage along the fence line.

I'm not sure I believe it was only from blood and bone."

"That could be the source, but so could the kitty litter from the school. Actually, no. Cat faeces gives a different form which doesn't match Nigella's pathology."

"But that puts us in a legal quandary about what I can charge Arlene with."

"Well, a non-legal, but medical perspective is that Fullers earth isn't toxic. It can cause mild gastric irritation, but I don't think it would kill you. But she wasn't taking it to kill herself. Quite the opposite in fact."

"Which means I'm going to need you to be really clear on what the cause of death was," Brad said.

"I know," Samantha replied.

"It's murder if eating the soil caused her death, but only if Nigella eating it was a reasonably foreseeable response to the poisoner's actions, but it's unlikely the mother had any clue about how she was surviving. It's murder if the poison killed her. But if it was the typhoid, it'd be near impossible to say that was an expected consequence. So that leaves attempted murder for the poisoning. But that doesn't seem fair. Nigella was killed because her mother planned for and gave her poison. That's unequivocally murder. Charging her with attempt when she'll likely get away with half the sentence seems wrong."

"But that's where there's the most likely conviction."

"I know, and if we go for murder, but they find someone who says the cause of death was typhoid, not ARDS, then the murder charge gets thrown out, she walks, and then it becomes much harder to charge her with the lesser crime."

"That's the sort of dilemma I'm glad I don't have to decide."

"No, but I'll need you to be very clear on cause of death. It's so dumb though. If we prosecute and fail for a higher charge, it undermines the possibility of conviction for a lesser one."

"That's where there's an art to what you do."

"I didn't appreciate that when I started. I do now." Brad raised his eyebrows, turned his palms upwards and slightly spread his arms. "Something still puzzles me. Why wouldn't she tell someone? Or get help?"

"The diary says she wanted to give her mum a chance to stop. Besides, all she had were suspicions. She was taking an antidote, so wasn't getting sick from the poison until the end. How could she be sure it wasn't all in her head? If she did tell, then her mum would have a pretty strong case for calling out her thinking as delusional or maybe even schizoid. She might even try to wrest control over the money as her daughter was mentally unfit. But, yeah, it also explains why her mum wouldn't take her to the doctor – they might realise she'd been poisoning her."

"What was the mum like when you spoke to her?"

"Remember, I was only asking about potential sources of contamination and epidemiology, so she had no reason to think I was suspicious of her, and indeed I wasn't at that time. She was shaky and distressed and seemed very unhappy, though I put that down to grief. She looked grief stricken."

"Maybe that was because things didn't go according to her plan."

"Probably. Though don't forget she lost a husband a few years ago and was left with a daughter who was her dependent, despite not being her child. She had to single-parent all through the most challenging stages of adolescence. She used to be an engineer. If you had a bitter disposition from having to give up your career and then losing your left thumb in an accident like she had, wouldn't you wish for a carefree life? If she could get Nigella's money and rid herself of Nigella, she'd be free."

Brad sighed. "Let me know when you've concluded how Nigella died."

"Will do."

"I'll go check out the school again. Maybe the maintenance guy, Terry, saw something? We didn't speak to him before."

"Good idea."

~

Brad was able to talk to Terry in the maintenance sheds at the school. It didn't take long for Brad to understand why Tiffany had described him as 'icky'. It wasn't the dirt, which was to be expected it was the general appearance and mannerisms which made the assessment appropriate. Terry had dried food round his mouth and in his stubble. He smelt of a few days' worth of stale body odour and his clothes were wrinkled and dirty.

"Tell me about the cat you look after," Brad said.

Terry's lined face suddenly brightened.

"She's a good kitty. She comes to see me most days. I look after her as best I can." Terry indicated the section of the workshop where there was a kitty litter tray, food and water bowl and an old towel which had been fashioned into a makeshift cat bed. Brad noticed the kitty litter had been used and was in need of a change. Terry saw it too and while he spoke to Brad, he took the tray and emptied it into a bin. Some dust flew up as the contents poured out. Terry sneezed into his hands and wiped them on his shirt. Brad frowned.

"She's come to see me for the last six months. You could say she's adopted me," Terry said proudly.

Terry pulled out a bag of kitty litter and used his hands to transfer several hand-scoopfuls into the tray. Brad observed the action and wondered if maybe Terry was the source of the typhoid rather than some contaminated soil. If he was a carrier for the disease and didn't wash his hands after going to the toilet, which seemed the sort of thing he would do, then wiping his bottom could transfer the bacteria to his hands and then to the kitty litter which Nigella ate.

"Would you excuse me a moment?" Brad asked. He walked a few metres away from the shed and called Samantha. He quickly explained what he was thinking.

"The thing is, at best, all I can collect right now is a urine sample. Will that be enough, or do you need to come down here and collect some blood and stool?"

"Urine could be enough. We can start with that and progress from there if necessary."

"Good."

Brad returned to his car and collected a sample jar. He returned to the maintenance shed. Thankfully, Terry was okay with providing a urine sample as long as it wasn't going to be tested for pot.

~

It didn't take long for Samantha to get back to Brad after re-examining the body and the additional pathology results from the body and Terry's urine. Terry did appear to be the source of the typhoid. Samantha suggested he was an asymptomatic carrier, much like Typhoid Mary had been. In her opinion, Nigella had died from typhoid, but only because her lungs were so weakened by the paraquat poisoning. She'd added that another examiner might reach the *vica versa* conclusion. The result confirmed Brad's suspicion. In order to give justice the greatest chance to be served, he'd have to charge Arlene with the lesser charge of attempted murder. Such a conclusion rankled him, but he needed to use the energy of that consternation to make sure no stone was left unturned in getting the conviction. The next step was to arrest the Arlene.

~

To Brad's surprise Arlene did not resist the arrest, though she did ask the charge. "I'm arresting you for the attempted murder of your daughter, Nigella."

"I didn't murder her. She was just a stupid girl." She acknowledged her rights and asked for her lawyer. The case proceeded to trial due to Arlene pleading innocent.

Brad arranged to attend the first day of the trial. All his

necessary statements had already been given by affidavit, so he was able to sit in.

Watching Arlene's face drop as the prosecutor discussed the diary and detailed its contents during their introduction was a moment Brad would remember fondly. The prosecutor did a stellar job in selling the evil stepmother trope. When it came time for the defence to try to counter with the evidence from Arlene's social media, it was too late, the jury's mind had already been conditioned to view it from the perspective of someone setting up an alibi. The wills of Nigella and her father clearly showed the pathway for the money to flow to Arlene. Combined with testimony from Tiffany that Nigella liked parties, but wasn't much of a drinker, the case was watertight. After all the arguments, it took the jury half a day to return a guilty verdict. Two months later Arlene was sentenced to twenty years imprisonment, with the possibility of parole after ten. Brad told himself to be satisfied that at least a measure of justice had been served.

Pressure Point

It was a cool, autumn, Monday morning when Sergeant Brad Thomas felt the familiar buzz of his phone. The only thief he knew socially was calling him, rather than the other way around. That had never happened before. When the phone rang, Brad put his post-run smoothie on his kitchen bench to free his hands to answer.

"Greetings," Brad said.

"Sarge, is there any chance we could talk today?" Jimmy 'Mug' Punter asked. His voice sounded strained. Mug was a friend of Brad's mentor, Dr Engels and an occasional informant. They usually started their conversations with a reminder not to mention any criminal activity.

"We are talking," Brad said jovially. He flicked the switch on the coffee machine. It seemed like he'd need one.

"I mean face to face, smartass."

Brad tried to conceal a sigh. He'd been looking forward to tuning out in front of replay of a motor race from the day before. And since he'd already been out for an hour-long run, his wife, Amy, wouldn't be happy if he went out again before his shift started at 1.00 pm.

"Hang on. I'll check with my wife. She's got a rostered day off."

"Sure. I'd do the same … if I had one. Happy wife, happy life."

Brad pressed the mute button, recalling his childhood where you'd put your hand over the mouthpiece, usually ineffectively. Technology was wonderful.

"Ames, can I go out to play?" He explained who Mug was and that he wanted to talk.

"Invite him here. I'd like to meet him. I mean, what does a thief look like?"

"In his case it's a short, fit, fifty-ish, man. He's a character."

Brad unmuted the phone. "Uh, Mug, how about you come here? You can meet my wife, Amy, and we can talk privately."

"Fine. Where are you?"

Brad gave Mug the address.

"I'll be there in twenty."

~

Mug was clearly nervous in Brad and Amy's apartment. His eyes kept darting around as though he was expecting someone to leap out at him. Amy had abruptly changed her mind about meeting Mug and gone for a walk. Brad served Mug a double espresso and sat opposite him at the kitchen table.

"What's up?" Brad asked.

132

"Sorry. I just feel weird visiting the home of a copper. Y'know? I'd hate to be seen."

Brad shrugged. "You asked to come here."

"The reason I'm here is that I need your help, unofficially though. You can't bring the police in on this."

Brad frowned with concern. "What's going on?"

"I've, uh, been seeing this woman, Ajna. She's an artist, but not just any artist. Her stuff just produces an emotional response. It's good. Sorry, I'm rambling. She has flair."

"And?"

"And, she's disappeared."

"Oh. Her name though, is your dyslexia…"

"Doc told you about that, huh. I wondered that too, no, her name is not Anja, it's Ajna. Anyway, yesterday morning there was a knock at my front door, and an envelope was slid underneath it. By the time I got there, there was no one there."

"So Ajna is living with you?"

"Sometimes. It was a plain white envelope, with only Ajna written on it. I handed it to her when she came out for breakfast. She opened it and pulled out a sheet of paper, gasped, and then when silent for a bit. She grabbed her stuff and left a few minutes later, only mumbling a goodbye. I haven't heard from her since, nor has she responded to my calls."

"Do you have the letter?"

Mug reached into his pocket and pulled out a crumpled envelope. "I took it out of the rubbish bin. You're not going to like it."

Brad opened the envelope and pulled out a plain indigo sheet of paper. He turned it over but couldn't see anything of interest.

"I don't get it. It's blank. What's so upsetting about that?"

"Told you, you wouldn't like it. That's my thought too. I can only think it's a secret code."

"Like the five orange pips?" Brad said.

"Yeah, something like that."

"I've never heard of a blank sheet of paper being used as a warning, or a threat."

"We've only been, um, dating for a couple of months, but I'm… I'm… I haven't told her how I feel yet."

Brad reached across the table and touched Mug's shoulder. "It's okay, there haven't been any Jane Doe's in the last day or two, so she's probably okay, but why can't the police be involved?"

"I haven't told you what she does. She teaches art at Mount Hawthorn College, but on the side she dabbles in stuff more related to my extracurricular activities."

"She steals to order?"

"No, she's a forger. Not anything like money, driver's licences, or passports, but let's say you need an official looking certificate or an ID card to get into a building. She's your gal."

"Ah, now I see why you like her. Artsy, clever and a little bit dark."

"How'd you know about clever?"

"Somehow I can't see you feeling that way about

someone you couldn't discuss ideas with. And it must be nice having someone you can talk freely about your deeds to. Besides, you're friends with Doc. He doesn't suffer fools. I can see you being the same."

Mug nodded. "If the police get involved and certain questions are asked, like why a group might want to kidnap her, if that's what's happened, then it could get her into trouble."

"Yeah. I can see why you want this off the books. My first thought is that someone may have taken her to create a licence or passport or something similar."

"I told you she doesn't do those."

"Yes, but if all someone wanted was what she normally forges then they'd pay her for it. No, if they've taken her then it must be for something she doesn't normally do."

Brad pulled out his phone. "I'm just going to do a search for indigo paper and hidden meanings. Maybe it'll point to a local group?"

"I've tried, but go ahead. You might catch something I missed."

Brad tapped away on his phone. A minute later, he sighed. "There's nothing. Just stuff on the history of indigo dye. That colour seems quite rare in nature. Though I had no idea there was an indigo mushroom which, for want of a better way of describing it, bleeds an indigo milk."

"Latex. The fluid is called latex."

Brad raised his eyebrows.

"What? Just 'cos I have certain interests doesn't mean I don't have others … but yeah, I read that article too."

"Fair enough. I can try to sneak a 'find my phone' kind of search for her. Can you give me her number?"

A clearly prepared Mug took a folded piece of paper out of his pocket and passed it to Brad.

"What about friends or family?"

"She's part of an artist group, which meets monthly. I don't know about family. It hasn't come up. I think maybe there's a brother or sister, but we try to keep things about us, not those around us."

"A special relationship then."

Mug nodded. "She was worried. I haven't seen that in her before. As I said, she left without her usual goodbye and hasn't responded to any attempt at contact for over a day. Normally she replies within ten minutes."

Brad reached across the table and placed a hand on Mug's shoulder. "Don't worry. We'll find her, and she'll be okay, you'll see."

"How can you be so sure?"

"The indigo paper was clearly a warning, or threat. Regardless, if someone wanted her dead then that's what she'd be. Instead, they gave her a chance to make things right, otherwise why send such a thing? Maybe that's what she's doing and it's just taking a bit of time." Brad spoke as confidently as he could, even though the situation worried him.

Mug looked Brad in the eye. "I want to believe you're right."

~

When he arrived at the station Brad grabbed a coffee, then

went straight to his office. The small room was barely big enough for a desk and chairs, but it was a private space at least. He pulled out the paper and stared at it. Maybe it was one of those magic eye things? Brad tried staring through the image, unfocusing his eyes and quickly glancing around the page, but nothing produced any effect. There had to be something more to it, and that was annoying. Not knowing, not seeing what others could, bothered him. It was an old bugbear he'd mostly worked through by improving his own observation skills and thinking, but that didn't stop his old feelings of inadequacy resurfacing.

Brad's inspection of the page was interrupted by a couple of taps on his door. A moment later, one of his detectives, Sally Summers, walked in and slumped in a chair opposite Brad. She was carrying a tablet computer.

"Boss, I've got a problem."

"You and me both."

Sally raised an eyebrow. "I'll tell you mine if you tell me yours."

"Deal, though I may not be able to give you more than the basics."

"I'm already intrigued, so here's mine. I have a victim of two assaults. He's late forties, very fit and apparently an expert martial artist."

"Oh yeah, what style?"

"I keep forgetting you were into that stuff."

"Not so much recently, but yeah."

"The vic is named Stan 'the man' Walker. He died after the second attack. Samantha sent me images she took

before the autopsy. He has bruises which are as dark as" –
Sally pointed to the paper on the desk – "as that paper.
What's up with that?"

"Nah-ah, you tell me first, remember?"

"Fine. Stan was attacked at 1.34 am in his dojo.
Someone came in and they talked for a bit. It got heated,
then they started fighting. It's all on CCTV."

"That early in the morning? I mean night? No
morning."

"It seems they'd planned the meeting. It doesn't seem
to have been with the intent to fight, as only Stan was in a
karate uniform."

"*Gi*."

"Okay *gi*, whatever, anyway they fought. Both walked
out of there, one much later than the other, but still, both
walked out. Perhaps due to the unknown guy putting Stan
in the recovery position. But, and this is where it gets
weird."

"Go on," Brad implored.

"The unknown guy came back that afternoon."

"What time?"

"About 5.30 pm. Stan's website said he had a class
starting at 6.00 pm."

"Why'd the attacker go back?"

"I'm not sure, but he did. They spoke for a minute then
started fighting again. This time Stan was struck hard in the
chest. He fell to his knees, but otherwise stayed up this
time. The unknown guy turned and left with a smug grin.
He held up two fingers as he left."

"Saying he'd beaten him twice?"

"That's what I thought. Anyway, Stan died a day and a half later. He was found this morning. Samantha did the autopsy straight away as a favour."

"Cause of death?"

Sally flicked through a few pages of the report she was holding. "Thrombosis. But an acute one. It seems to have affected the super vena cava, which meant the deoxygenated blood couldn't return to the heart. He had facial swelling, a venous distention in the neck and distended veins in the upper chest and arms. There was a lot of fluid build-up around his upper body. His heart didn't receive enough blood, so he slowly lost consciousness and died."

"Slowly?"

"The report indicates he must've taken about thirty hours to die. They found him at his home. He missed a class he was meant to teach, so the alarm was raised."

"Which takes us to right back to the time he was attacked."

"Exactly. Hence an investigation."

"We caught a break by having it caught on the dojo's security system. Stan was logged into the feed when they found him at his home. Probably studying where he went wrong. We got the files from the cloud."

"Can I see?"

Sally opened her laptop and brought up two video files, then added them to a playlist.

The first video showed Stan alone in his dojo. He

appeared to be drinking a beer. A plain-clothed man entered. They had a conversation, which became more and more animated, before Stan threw a punch at the man, who stepped forward, twisted to the side and pushed Stan backwards. Stan stumbled, then fell on his bottom."

Brad laughed. "Dude doesn't know how to fight. How is he a martial art instructor?"

"Keep watching."

Stan stood and launched another angry attack. This time he caught the other man on the cheek as he was stepping to the side and behind Stan. The blow was only glancing though, and while it would probably have left a graze on the cheek, it wasn't sufficient to stun him, nor alter his motion. The defender grabbed Stan's black ponytail and pulled his head back. He jammed his thumb underneath Stan's collarbone and stomped on Stan's foot. Stan dropped to his knees as his defender turned assailant finished with a dropped elbow to the centre of Stan's forehead. Stan was clearly knocked out cold from the attack. To Brad's surprise, the unknown man immediately put Stan in the recovery position and picked up what appeared to be Stan's phone and made a call."

"That was to the emergency services," Sally said. "They sent out a paramedic, but when they got there Stan had regained consciousness. The idiot refused treatment and sent them away. The unknown guy had left once Stan started coming round."

Sally skipped to the next video.

This time it was clearly daylight. The quality of the

image was much less grainy. There was another animated conversation between the two men. Again, Stan struck first. This time the unknown man stepped inside the punch, grabbed Stan's wrist with his left hand and stunned Stan with a jab to his eyes. As Stan reflexively drew his hands to his face, the defender moved his left hand to grip Stan's palm, then gave a peculiar punch which seemed to lead with the tip of his thumb, striking Stan on the chest. Stan stumbled backwards, before recovering and moving forwards. He appeared to think twice, and just waved the unknown man out of the dojo. He dropped to his knees.

"The bruise from that was such a dark blue. I've never seen anything like it. It wasn't to the heart, like I first thought after seeing the video. It was higher, about the third rib or so."

"Anything strike you as odd about the two attacks?"

"What do you mean?"

"The second time the unknown guy attacked different parts of Stan. That seems odd. I mean Stan effectively gave the same attack of a right hook both times, so why didn't the guy use the same defence?"

"Do you always defend the same way?"

"I guess not. We've got good footage of him, so run his face through facial recognition and see if there's a hit. Maybe we can call him in for an interview and get more details."

"James is running it for me now," Sally said.

"Good. Let me know when you're interviewing the guy. There's something about it I can't quite put my finger on.

I studied Shotokan karate throughout my teenage years. It's a very linear style, you know, forward backward side to side kind of thing. The attacker seems to be using more body shift than that style. Maybe a Ninjitsu or Wado student? They emphasise that kind of shift. I know there's a great Wado school in Geraldton, and there used to be one in John Forrest. Could be Goju. They also do a lot of in-close fighting. It didn't look like he was using one of the internal arts, like *tai chi* or *bagua*, though that thumb-driven punch seems like he's targeting very specific points. If you get a recognition match, do a web search on the name with sensei in front. I'd bet you'll get a hit."

"Can do, but you're distracting me."

"From what?"

"The indigo paper."

"Oh yeah, I'd kinda forgotten about that. It was sent to a woman yesterday morning. She took a brief look at it and totally freaked out. She left the place she was in and hasn't been seen or heard from since."

"Why? What does it mean?"

"That's the mystery. Any ideas?"

"Not a clue. It's a plain sheet of paper. Does the colour mean something?"

"Not to me, nor to anyone else as far as the web search revealed."

"So … check in together in a couple of hours?"

"A great idea."

Brad smiled as Sally left his office. She liked the mystery as much as he did. Though something about her case bugged Brad.

~

Brad decided to take a walk around the block of the police station. It wasn't a long path, but the fifteen minutes it would take would give him a chance to clear his head. He hoped no one would notice his absence so soon into his shift. As he stepped outside, the sunlight blinded his eyes. It took a moment for his eyes to adjust once he started his walk. He passed a community garden and appreciated the sight of many bees flying between flowers. What would a bee detect in a crime scene with their ability to see into the UV range? It would be a cool ability but, as Brad knew from a past case, if a human wanted that ability they'd have to sacrifice their ability to focus. That was too big a price in Brad's mind. Still, it would be cool to flit around and see what others couldn't. A bee could see things from all sorts of angles and heights others couldn't. The extra patterning on flowers they saw always seemed so impressive in the images Brad had seen. That gave him an idea. Maybe there was something hidden in Mug's indigo paper like that, so only visible to certain people. Brad had already shone a UV torch on it, so it wasn't another case of aphakia, but still, there could be something.

By the time Brad returned to his desk, he had a clear plan of action. He scanned the indigo paper and opened the image in his computer. He changed the colour selector to show the CMYK sliders and selected the eyedropper tool. It was on the eleventh click the cyan slider took a small jump to the left. Brad noted the location and clicked a few more times. It took another five clicks before a similar jump occurred. Brad went to the menu and selected the colour range tab. A moment later all instances of the skewed colour were being bordered by a black and white striped selection frame. The outlines formed letters, which spelled out the message *Need help. Bring your tools. PLEASE @dojo – S*

Brad pushed back in his chair and stood. Then looked at the screen again. Could there possibly be a link between Mug's girlfriend's disappearance and Detective Summer's case? It seemed too incredulous to be possible, yet the reference to a dojo was surely more than mere coincidence? And the 'S' seemed to seal the connection.

Could Ajna be at the dojo? Brad called Sally into his office and asked for its address. Sally gave it to him and added, "I've found the unknown guy. He's Sensei Kratos Hobbs. He runs a dojo in Duncraig. He's on his way in."

"Cool, hopefully I'll be back in time to see him. As it stands it'd be hard to charge him with anything. Maybe a low-level assault charge, but if his explanation is self-defence, the video corroborates that. Plus, he phoned for help and put him in recovery that first time. The second time he left Stan standing. I'm going to see if there's anyone at Stan's dojo."

Sally pointed to the screen message. "Don't ask. I don't know what it means, at least not yet," Brad said.

On his way out, he turned to Sally. "There's something about the defences he used that's bugging me, but I can't work out what it is. Something about the change of target and their apparent specificity."

~

The dojo was located in a strip of warehouse-style shops. Brad hoped Stan's fight left him disoriented enough to forget to turn on the alarm. Though, if someone was trapped inside it would have gone off by now, but still Brad wanted to avoid a scene if it sounded. There was still the matter of the lock. Brad knelt at the door and took out his lock-picking kit. It was something he rarely used, but it had come in handy from time to time. It was much nicer than smashing a door down to execute a warrant. After a minute of careful manipulations, the lock sprung back. Brad turned the handle and entered the dojo. He may not have a warrant, but if things went awry he could claim to be investigating a missing person case, despite the awkward questions it might raise for Mug.

The hall was sparsely decorated. There was a black and white picture of an old karate master on the wall and a rack, usually used for pool cues, which had several *bos* placed in it. The floor was made up of pink and blue foam mats, forming an intricate pattern. Brad recognised the one kanji he knew in the pattern – *wa* – the word for harmony. As he stepped across the room, Brad noticed another framed image on the side of the wall he'd entered from. It was of a Bible verse, "Psalms 18:39: For you have girded me with strength for battle; you have subdued those who rose up against me". Brad thought about the irony of the Bible celebrating the death of others, as surely the 'subdued' implied. Then he froze. That was it. The quote triggered the memory he'd been searching for when viewing the videos of the attacks. With a start Brad realised he might have a case of murder on his hands after all. He sent a message to Sally to hold Kratos until Brad returned to the station, which he'd do ASAP. He also asked her to print him three specific images from the videos of the fights between Stan and Kratos.

Brad listened for any signs of an alarm. It seemed odd calling out in an empty, echoey hall, but Brad still shouted, "Ajna, are you here?"

Brad wasn't sure if it was relief, surprise or excitement he felt when he heard a muffled cry of, "I'm here."

The sound came from a side room next to a small kitchenette. Brad ran over, despite feeling a little silly as it didn't feel like an emergency.

"The door's locked. It's keyed on both sides. I can't get out," Ajna said as Brad tried the handle.

"Give me a minute."

Brad took out his lock-picking kit and within a minute had the door unlocked. He opened it to reveal what was barely more than a storeroom. It was cluttered with martial arts equipment from pads to weapons. There was a small desk, upon which was laid out a framed certificate stating that someone named Daryl Hawkins was a fifth Dan in their martial art style. Next to it was a perfect replica with the name replaced by 'Stan Walker.' Two mugs were on the desk, each seemed to have water in them. Beside the desk was a black suitcase. In the corner of the room was a tall, thin woman with hair that was jet black save for a blue streak at the front. Her artful use of make-up accentuated the brightness of her eyes and shape of her lips. She wore a knitted top which showed off her shapely figure.

"Ajna?" Brad asked.

"Yes. How do you know who I am?"

"I've been looking for you. Look, I'm sorry to rush this but can we get going? I need to get something from my house and get back to the station."

"You're a cop?"

Brad looked at his shirt and tie and realised it wasn't obvious. "Yes. But don't worry, I'm not here to talk to you about your, uh, copying."

"Okaaay."

"I take it you've been trapped in here for a day or so?"

"Yes. Don't drink the water. It isn't water. At least not anymore."

"Oh."

"I wasn't desperate enough to drink that yet. I figured someone would turn up sooner or later. Where's my brother? Did he get locked up again?"

So that was how she'd rationalised a policeman coming to rescue her. Stan must have been her sibling. "I'm afraid not. He … he died yesterday."

"Oh." Ajna seemed to take the news with only a slight indication of sadness. In what Brad assumed was a response to his questioning look, she said, "We were never close. He only contacted me for money or when he wanted something. I've come to his aid a lot over the years because he's family, but only because of that. How'd he die?"

"A blockage of a vein above his heart."

"Oh, I thought you were going to say in a fight."

"We know he'd been in a couple of fights recently."

"That's why he wanted me to … err … reproduce his certificate. He wanted to show his doubters that he was legit."

"Only a Mug Punter would believe he was legit."

Ajna's head twitched. "I have to make a call. But I accidentally left my phone in my car at the train station."

"Don't worry, his number's in my phone. I'll get him to meet you at my place."

"How? What? You seem to know me. I'm so confused."

"I'll explain on the way. Can we please get going? Bring your tools." Brad nodded to the suitcase.

~

After a call to a very relieved Mug, Brad drove Ajna and himself to his apartment. There was a bible he needed to check.

"So, what's the deal with the piece of paper you saw at Mug's? How on earth could you read the message?" Brad asked.

"How could you?" Ajna replied.

"I scanned it and found the colour difference of the words and highlighted them."

"I don't have to do that. I can just read them."

"That makes no sense."

"You know how your eyes have three colour receptors, red, blue and green. Some people have one less – they're colour blind."

"Yes."

"Well, I have a fourth one. It means I can see many millions more shades than the average person. I can read the writing on that page easily. My brother knew that. It's a better means of concealing a message than any code."

"Does he have the same ability?"

"No. He's a he. The bonus genes are on the X chromosome and you need two mismatched sets for it to work. I can't see beyond normal colour vision though, just more variation in the colour spectrum."

"Is that why you're an artist?"

"Not directly. I think it helps my art appeal to people though. It appears more aesthetic, even though people can't quite say why. I match colours better to life. You still haven't told me how Mug is friends with a copper."

"I'm an acquaintance. We've met a couple times through a mutual friend who likes having a circle of people from different walks of life. I'm sure there's a strategy to it, though I'm just not sure what yet. Mug was very concerned about you. I mean he reached out to me, which must've been hard for him to do."

"Cool."

"Cool?"

"Yeah. He really likes me."

"I'd say he's in l— smitten. You know he thinks you were kidnapped."

"Shit. No, just my idiot brother thought he should lock the door while he taught his morning class. They're all seniors and don't always know which door is which. I can't believe he left without unlocking it or talking to me."

"To be fair, he was probably feeling a bit out of it."

"Yeah." The emotion of losing her brother seemed to catch up to Ajna, and she turned her head towards the door in silence, but not before Brad had caught a glimpse of a tear rolling down her cheek. The anger at being trapped must have worn off.

Brad let the silence remain as he approached his apartment block. Amy would be home, which was convenient.

~

"Amy, this is Ajna. She's a friend of Mug's."

Amy rose from the couch where she'd been watching TV and greeted Ajna with a handshake. Brad was amused by the action between the women. In his hometown, handshakes were what men did. He hadn't been able to shake the notion, despite years of living in the city, even though it made sense when a kiss hello would be too familiar.

"Hi Ajna, I'm Amy. Can I get you a drink?"

"Tea?"

"I'll put the kettle on." Amy pressed the switch on the kettle then sat next to Ajna on the couch.

Brad went to search for the book he wanted. It wasn't on his bookshelf, and by the time he'd found it in the box of books he and Amy had never unpacked after moving in together, the kettle had boiled. He brewed a tea for Ajna and then said his goodbye, asking Amy to look after her until Mug had arrived to pick her up.

~

Brad sat in his car and flicked through the book until he found the chapter he was after. When he read it he knew Kratos had murdered Stan. He just needed one detail to confirm it. Brad phoned the medical examiner, Samantha, and explained what he was thinking. "Brachiocephalic vein compression is often indistinguishable from SVC obstruction. So, yes, it's possible that was the manner of death, and I can see how that could be caused the way you're talking about," she said.

Brad tried to keep to the limit as he drove to the station. He wasn't responding to an emergency call, so he would be subject to the same punishment for infringing as everyone else, but as he drove he saw the telltale double flash of a speed camera.

~

Once at the station, Brad went straight to the interview room where Sally was talking to Kratos. Kratos was intimidating, not because of his size, he wasn't much larger than Brad, nor because of his appearance, which was clean shaven with a military style haircut. It was the way he held himself. Brad knew from the videos Kratos knew how to fight, but here in the room it was apparent just from his posture as he sat and the way his eyes focused to take in the room. Brad was pleased he'd thought to place the book in his laptop bag before entering – Kratos would have noticed it straight away.

"Hi, Kratos, my name is Sergeant Thomas. I know

you've taken Detective Summers through your version of events, but could you please talk me through them too? Just a brief rundown. I've seen the videos and am familiar with the basics of the case. Stan's unfortunate passing so close to a fight means we have to consider whether charges need to be laid. It's standard protocol in these circumstances to have two officers work through the details."

That was only partly true. Two officers would sign off on the paperwork to rubber stamp the conclusion and provide some defence against accusations of bias, but it also wasn't unusual to work some parts of a case alone.

"Sure. Stan set up his dojo a few months ago. I don't know how he thought it would be a money-spinning machine. It's near impossible to make any more than a hobbiest income from it. He started trying to poach students from other dojos by placing flyers on cars while the owners were training. Then he started hanging out and trying to talk to people as they left. Let's just say he started to say some pretty terrible things about a few instructors to get students to defect to his dojo. He spread some pretty malicious lies and criticised styles."

"Isn't that what happens? Dojos fight each other?" Sally asked innocently.

"In 1970s movies, yeah maybe. But not in the real world. There may be some rivalry, but mostly amongst the instructors there's a respect born of understanding how hard it is to have done what we have, for as long as we have, to get to where we are. Besides, at the moment all us traditional practitioners are bleeding students to mixed martial arts. We couldn't afford to lose more to some blowhard who couldn't fight his way out of a wet paper bag."

"That's a very unfortunate position. Stan must have upset you greatly. Is that why you went to his dojo? To discuss with him how to make amends?" Brad asked. His empathy was designed to engineer a rapport, which he could then use to his advantage. Kratos picked up on the hint in Brad's question.

"Yes, that's exactly why I went there. I wanted him to stop badmouthing myself and some instructor friends of mine."

Brad took out his laptop and started playing the video of the first fight.

"Why was it so late at night?"

"That's when Stan wanted it to be. I guess he wanted no one else around."

"Why?"

"I dunno. Maybe he thought there could be a fight and he didn't want anyone to witness it if he lost. Deep down he must have known that would be the likely outcome. I knew that too; that's why when he started talking back, I tried to get him to stop and show reason. Look there, see I hold my arms up and take a step back. I was trying to get him to calm down."

Brad paused the video. "What style do you do? I studied Shotokan for a while. I made it to first kyu."

"One off black belt. That's well done. I'm a goju-ryu

practitioner, so we wouldn't know any of the same kata even though our founders shared the same instructors."

Brad nodded and resumed the video.

"So here Stan is getting angry because I threatened to complain to the police about him slandering us. I said if one more bad thing was said about any of the other schools, I'd personally see to it he was exposed as a fraud. The jackass said he'd bring his 5th Dan certificate in the next day. I said he was lying, and he took offence and swung at me. I put him down. Then when I realised how bad he was hurt, I put him in the recovery position and called an ambulance."

The video matched Kratos' version of events. Brad skipped to the second fight.

"That was good of you. What happened here?" Brad asked.

"I went back that afternoon to see his alleged certificate. He didn't have it, though he swore black and blue he'd have it the next day. I again accused him of being a fraud and not knowing true martial arts. He swung at me, and I defended myself. This time I left him standing, well, on his knees but upright."

"What was your intent when he swung at you?" Brad asked. This was crucial for determining whether a charge could be laid.

"Defence. I reacted on instinct."

Brad paused the video just as Kratos held up two fingers.

"Both your responses last no more than a second or

two, so it's perfectly reasonable to accept you were acting instinctively. Once he dropped or was stopped you stopped too. So, it could be argued that you didn't respond disproportionately to his attack."

Kratos nodded. A hint of a smile flitted across his face.

"That's important. It means it's unlikely we need to press charges against you," Sally said.

Kratos visibly exhaled.

"Except for one thing," Brad said softly. He reached into his laptop bag and pulled out his book. Brad tried to keep his voice even, though this was the moment he loved most about being a police officer – trapping the suspect and showing them they had been *caught*. "This is the bible of karate, the *Bubishi*. I was given a copy to study on my journey towards black belt. Something bugged me watching the videos. It was the way you changed the position of your hand the second time, so you were gripping the middle of his palm. You already had his wrist, so there was no need for it, unless there was some other purpose. Plus, the difference in your defences and the specific targeting of the strikes bothered me. Most times in a fight like that you'd strike the head going for a knock-out or jab the eyes or something, but you targeted the collarbone the first time and not the heart, but between the thyroid and the heart. So, I went and dug out the *Bubishi* to clarify my distant memory."

Brad slid over the first photo he'd had Sally print. It was a photo of Stan. On it he'd drawn some dots where Kratos had struck.

"Here's what I read in chapter twenty-one: Ox (1.00-3.00 am). Death within 14 days can be caused by traumatising the carotid artery and sublingual nerve, which is located between the sternomastoid muscle and the collarbone bone – but only when the head is being tilted back by pulling on the hair, the external calcean artery on the outer ankle, or the anterior temporal artery just below the hairline."

Brad turned the book round and pointed to the sketched image of a man with the points labelled on it. He pointed to the corresponding points on the photo of Stan.

"Those are the exact points you struck, and the time of the first fight was right at the start of that time range."

Kratos' face fell during Brad's reading. His confidence seemed to wash off his being and he slumped in his chair. Brad slid across the second, similarly marked photo.

Brad continued. "Rooster (5.00-7.00 pm). Death within two days can be caused by severe trauma to the left innominate vein at the third intercostal space, while depressing the deep ulnar artery in the centre of the palm between the third and fourth metacarpal. The fight was at 5.30 pm."

Brad pointed to the third photo, which was of Kratos holding up two fingers. "That's not you saying two victories. That's you saying two days to live. Stan died thirty hours later."

"So?" Stan said glumly.

"I conferred with the person who did the autopsy. She said his cause of death was consistent with such an attack.

You knew you were killing him."

"You can't prove that," Kratos said, but it was clear it was bluster.

"Yes, I can. But do you want to know the real kicker?"

"What?"

"It was your own testimony that betrayed you. That's poor defence."

Kratos looked confused. "I don't see how."

"You didn't go back the next day to see the certificate. Why? Because you knew he'd be dead or dying."

"I did," Kratos said unconvincingly.

"No, you didn't," Sally said triumphantly. "There's no footage of you there. I watched all the way through to this morning." Brad was grateful for her ability to switch mode from 'getting a statement' to 'interviewing a *suspect*'.

"I stayed in the corner. No one was there. I called out and everything."

"No, you didn't," Brad said. "And I know that because there was a person trapped in the building at the time, who would have loved for someone to hear them."

Kratos sunk deeper into his chair.

"Fine. I did it. I knew he'd die. He knew nothing about the art of defence. He couldn't even attack without leaving himself wide open. It was like fighting a white belt."

"Thank you for admitting it. For that, I'll reward you with the satisfaction of knowing he was a fraud. The person who was trapped in the building was there to fake a Dan certificate for him."

Kratos shook his head. "The fucker."

~

After booking Kratos, Brad and Sally went to his office.

"Care to explain what that was all about? Death within certain timeframes, but only if the strikes are done within certain hours of the day?"

"I know it sounds like hooey. And the prosaic name for such techniques being 'the touch of death', or *Dim Mak*, gives such techniques a mystique which is underserved. Really, they are fancy ways of traumatising the body to cause death and show a good understanding of human anatomy and physiology given they come from such an old document. But I had Sam confirm they'd work in the manner described, especially if no treatment was provided."

"What are you going to do with the witness?" Sally asked. The question was innocent, but Brad knew he now had a dilemma about what to do with Ajna. If he asked her to testify, he'd be betraying the one request of Mug's to keep the police out of it, but he needed it to round off the case, even with the confession. Brad realised Ajna's testimony was only relevant as far as showing Stan was operating without any real authority. Perhaps it could be twisted that she was reached out to, as a renowned artist, for help? Maybe Stan told her all she was doing was reproducing a lost original? They were estranged enough for it to be feasible. He nodded to himself as he concluded he could just get a sworn statement that she was accidentally trapped in the building and no one had been there before Brad arrived.

"I'll take care of that," Brad said as his phone dinged with a text. It was a message from Mug. *Thanks for finding Ajna. I might have underestimated how much people miss something when it's gone.;-)*

The White Tales

The offer from Brad's mentor Dr Engels arrived out of the blue, in the form of an early morning phone call as Brad was eating his breakfast. "I'm forming a group to meet for a meal and mystery twice a year, and I'd like you and Amy to take part."

"Uh, okay," Brad had replied.

"Your job for our first meeting is to bring a guest who you think could create a worthy mystery for the group's members to solve." The doctor explained he had been reading Azimov's stories of the *Black Widowers* recently and couldn't stop thinking about how much fun it might be to create a similar get-together of friends. The regulars would be: Brad, a detective; his wife Amy, a human resource manager; Jimmy 'Mug' Punter, a consultant thief; Dr Engels, entrepreneur and man of science: Gwyn Yang, romance author; and a sixth to be determined after a few guests had been through. The list had been cultivated for diversity. The aim was to have such a breadth of knowledge, experience and understanding of human behaviour, no mystery could withstand their combined scrutiny.

~

It hadn't taken Brad long to choose a guest for the evening. Samantha was a senior medical examiner and a good friend. She'd told Brad she'd spent a whole evening preparing the mystery, though the real difficulty was working out what case lore to base it on. In her job she'd certainly seen many unusual murders and deaths. But the most interesting ones had attracted some media coverage and it was likely either Brad or Dr Engels would know of them. Instead, she said she'd go old-school. A simple crime with a twist.

The group met at Dr Engels private residence in the Ivory Towers building in the city. The residence adjoined Dr Engels' company offices, which took up two of the upper floors of the building. After being shown through the secret entrance in Leviathan Enterprises entry foyer, the group was taken to Dr Engels' sitting room for canapes. While they mingled, Mug thanked Brad for his recent help in tracking down Mug's girlfriend after she had gone missing. The group was served by a waiter who had been hired for the evening. Unlike the Black Widowers, this waiter wasn't part of the group, nor expected to contribute to the proceedings.

After the main course of the best dhufish Brad had ever tasted, and a dessert of which the most ardent molecular gastronome would be proud, it was time for the night's main event.

Each guest had chosen their own malt whisky from Dr Engels' extensive collection. Brad had chosen a nice Speyside, Dr Engels and Samantha had whiskies from Islay, Amy had a whisky from the Isle of Skye with a side glass of water, and Gwyn had bucked the trend and poured a cognac instead.

They sat in a u-shaped arrangement on double-sized, cream-coloured leather sofas facing Samantha who was in an armchair opposite them. Brad and Amy shared one sofa, Dr Engels and Mug were on the middle one and Gwyn was on her own.

Dr Engels tapped his glass with a spoon. The clear tone produced immediately caused a hush.

"Thank you all for coming to what I hope will be the first of many such events. The evening will now turn to our main event, since we've eaten our desserts as per the Black Widowers who inspired this evening. I've served single malts in lieu of the outdated post-dinner brandy. I should also point out, unlike the Black Widowers, this group will contain women, the mystery can be made up, and there will be no requirement for the guest to justify their existence. Hence, I propose our name be the White Tales, as both a play on a spider's name and the storytelling."

There were several, "Hear, hears". Samantha clinked a glass with the doctor.

Gwyn grinned and said sardonically, "Well, if we're not going to be anything like them, why mention it?"

"He's an academic at heart. He likes to acknowledge his

sources," Brad replied with a laugh.

Dr Engels nodded to Brad, then repeated the action to Samantha. Samantha rose from her armchair.

"First of all, thank you for the invite. I've had a great time preparing my little puzzle for you, though it was not an easy task. I know how well regarded each of you are in your respected fields, and Doc, once again, sorry for thinking you were a murderer in a past life," Samantha said.

Dr Engels nodded and saluted with a sip of his whisky. That case had been Brad's first major investigation after he moved to the city.

"The mystery I'd like to present is of a woman I'll name Ramona. Ramona was staying with her husband, Pedro, at the Luxton Hotel, not far from here. They were celebrating their honeymoon. When they arrived, their affection for each other was noted by the person who signed them in. They seemed excited to be in Perth and asked in broken English about which beaches to visit and how to get to Kings Park. They were due to stay for three weeks. By the second week some waitstaff had observed a change in the dynamic between the two. Pedro seemed increasingly moody and agitated. The staff wondered if he was having regrets about the marriage. At the start of the third week, Ramona ran a bath, then took a bottle of champagne and smashed it over Pedro's head. He fell to the floor and she dragged him into the bath and held him under. He regained consciousness and fought violently. His cries caused guests in the neighbouring room to call reception, who sent the concierge to check on them. When the concierge got to the room, he heard agonised screaming. He let himself in and ran to the bathroom. He saw Ramona holding her husband under the water. As he went to pull her away, Pedro stopped thrashing. He'd drowned."

Dr Engels picked up a whiteboard marker and started making notes on a large, red, glass feature on the wall behind Samantha's armchair. He noted, 'broken English', 'honeymoon', 'champagne', 'bath' and 'drowned'.

"If any of you want to add to this, feel free," he said to the group. "Please continue, Sam."

"The concierge heard Ramona say what to him sounded like 'toove kay'. Another staff member swore she'd seen Pedro hit his bride at breakfast that morning and appear extremely agitated. It was thought Ramona had drowned him in retaliation.

"What I want to know is why, a week later, the detectives investigating the case dropped all charges against her?"

Amy jumped in with her reply. "Was it self-defence? I mean, if he was violent she could claim she was in fear for her life and was just protecting herself."

Brad glanced at Dr Engels. He looked crestfallen. If that was the solution his whole evening would be underwhelming, rather than the celebration of rationality he'd hoped for.

Samantha appeared to have noticed the look on the doctor's face too. "Aww, poor doctor, cheer up. That's not the solution. I wouldn't have brought you such a simple mystery. Though, Amy, I must say that was what I wanted people to leap to."

"So, was she in fear for her life or not?" Gwyn asked.

"No. She wasn't," Samantha replied.

"But he hit her."

"Yes."

"Was the witness mistaken?" Gwyn questioned.

"No. He really hit her."

"Was it an accident?"

"No, it was a proper strike, with the intent to harm—"

"So, why wouldn't they think self-defence?" Amy interjected.

"That's what I'm asking you," Samantha replied.

"Was anything stolen?" Mug asked.

"No."

"Were they really in love?" Gwyn asked.

Sam nodded. "Yes, hotel staff said when they arrived they seemed deliriously happy."

"Of course. They'd just got married," Amy said. She turned to Brad and smiled.

"And that's the happiest they'd ever be, even without the events Sam is describing," Dr Engels said with a wry grin.

"What? How can you possibly know that?" Amy asked.

"Simple. Research by Clark, Diener, and Georgellis on happiness shows a peak rating around the time of marriage. It's mostly downhill from there." He took a whiteboard marker and drew a graph on the glass board. "From memory the graph was something like this."

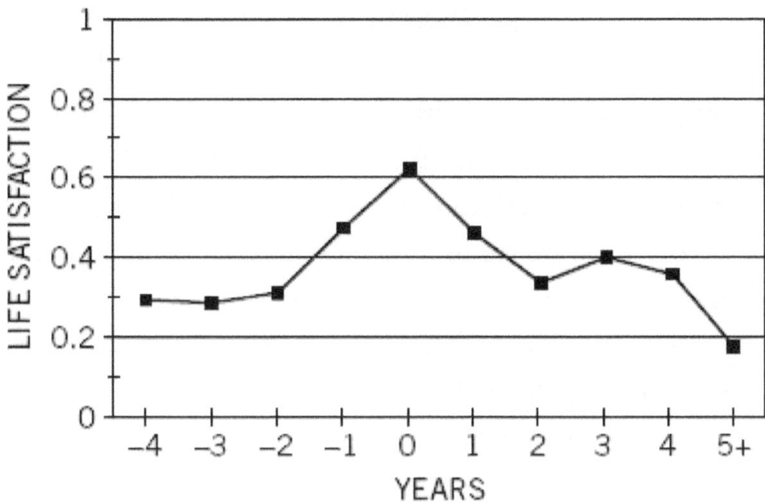

"It's why romance books end with a wedding. At least mine usually do," Gwyn said. "It's the happiest ending there can be."

"Can't say I've ever been asked by a newlywed to steal something," Mug chimed in.

"The time after the honeymoon is when the HR team has noticed people rate their contentment with us as their employer as the highest," Amy said. "I hadn't twigged about that meaning it was all downhill after that. Does that mean Brad and I aren't going to remain this happy?" Amy's expression changed to one of concern, and she looked accusingly at Brad. Brad read her expression as meaning if their happiness changed, it would be his fault.

"Now, now, you two," Dr Engels said with a mirthful chuckle. "The accuracy of this has been questioned. In particular, the Nobel Prize winner, Daniel Kahneman, showed the peak around the time of the wedding is due to an anchoring bias. Basically, you rate yourself as more satisfied with life because your first thought when you're asked for a rating is to think of your wedding. He showed you can make anyone feel closer to peak satisfaction, if, before asking them to rate their life, you asked someone to list things they're grateful for. That's also why thinking of three things you're grateful for or happy about at the end of each day is an effective strategy for happiness. In the past prayer could achieve this – you know, by giving thanks for the things your god had provided you. But since religion is on the wane, it now needs to be a deliberate practice. So, I say, anchor yourselves to your happiness by taking a few minutes to think about the things that bring you happiness each day."

"Are lectures on how to live going to be a regular feature of these nights?" Gywn asked sardonically.

Dr Engels flushed. "Sorry, I go off on tangents a little too easily. I'll be quiet now. Although, in my defence, having scientific support for our poor couple being happy could be important for figuring out why Ramona was released."

"How had the couple financed the trip?" Mug asked. "You said it was their honeymoon, but three weeks in a posh hotel on the other side of the world … actually, do we know where they're from?"

"I haven't said it," Samantha admitted.

"Are they Mexican?" Mug queried.

"Yes."

"So how did they afford the trip? You mentioned they wanted to go to the beach and walk around Kings Park. Those things are effectively free. Were they poor?" Mug asked.

"They weren't wealthy. You're right about that. The flights and first week of accommodation were part of a prize they'd won, and the remaining two weeks were paid for by their wedding guests in lieu of a present."

"Was Pedro afraid?" Dr Engels asked.

"He didn't want to be drowned. If that's what you mean. Nor was he afraid of Ramona."

"Any other marks on Pedro?" Mug asked.

"A few old scars, nothing fresh though," Samantha said.

"I can't help thinking you made the victim foreign for a reason," Brad said. "That extra detail is meant to be a clue, isn't it?"

Samantha smiled and shrugged nonchalantly. "Maybe."

"Are we allowed to look things up on our phones?" Amy asked.

"The Black Widowers were allowed to consult reference books. I guess it could be allowed, but only for certain facts. You can't go searching for 'How to get away with drowning someone' or similar," Dr Engels said.

"Okay, well, does anyone know what 'toove kay' translates to, or should I look it up?" Amy asked.

"It's meant to be *tuve que*. It's Spanish for 'I had to'," Mug said. The group looked at him in surprise. He shrugged. "What? Just because I'm a consultant thief doesn't mean I'm not a man of the world. I studied Spanish in high school. I can remember the odd phrase. That's one. *Lo sciento.* That's another. Quite useful too."

"Why would she feel she had to drown him? That seems odd," Amy said. "If Brad hit me, I wouldn't drown him. I'd divorce him and take him for everything I could."

"Aw, thanks, Hun," Brad said. He clasped her hand.

Amy glanced at her stomach and raised her head. "Was she pregnant?"

"No, why?"

"She might not have killed him to protect herself, but maybe she was defending her unborn baby? You said it wasn't self-defence, but was that a sly way of getting us to move past protection as a motive?"

"Good thinking, Amy," Dr Engels said admiringly.

"Thanks. Makes me feel better about jumping to the obvious conclusion before."

"Whether she was pregnant or not has no bearing on the incident," Samantha said.

"Though on that front, anything you want to tell us?" Mug interjected, talking to Amy. "Reading people is crucial in my line of work. You haven't been drinking your drink, Brad has. You've drunk only the water. You looked at your tummy before asking about pregnancy, as though it made you think of the question. Plus, you and Brad seem kinda snugly. Like you have a secret, but it's something good because you've maintained contact since you've got here. Even at dinner you shuffled your chairs closer to each other."

Brad realised he'd been resting his hand on Amy's leg and their knees had been touching for the whole of the presentation of the mystery.

Dr Engels had a hopeful glint in his eye. Samantha laughed.

"Yes, we're pregnant," Amy said with a grin.

"Whoohoo, finally I can talk to someone else about it," Samantha said.

"Congratulations," said everyone else simultaneously. Dr Engel's went to the bar fridge and took out a bottle of champagne, which Brad recognised as costing hundreds per bottle. Dr Engels poured half a glass for everyone, bar Amy, and handed them round.

"We're only four months, so let's not get ahead of ourselves. Besides, there are more pressing matters like this mystery. I want to solve it," Amy said.

"Me, too," Brad said. "So very quickly, we don't know if it's a boy or girl, but we are going to find out next week. We're due around September, but aren't giving the expected date as we want to surprise people when it happens."

"Got it. Back to the mystery then," Mug said.

Dr Engels smiled. "While I was pouring the drinks, I was thinking over what you've told us, Sam. You didn't give me a straight answer to my question about fear. You've had clear answers for everyone's questions bar that one. Was Pedro normally afraid of anything specifically?"

"No. Not normally." Brad realised Samantha's caginess meant the doctor was on to something.

"But was he afraid of a specific thing when he died?"

"Yes."

"As in hydrophobic?"

Samantha smiled. "This isn't chemistry. I think you mean aquaphobic and the answer is yes."

He *was* on to something, but for the life of him Brad couldn't figure out why being afraid of water was such an important clue.

"Which means, I think I know why she got away with it. You couldn't bring us something local, because Brad might have heard of a similar case."

Samantha nodded.

"You had to import something we don't have in Australia."

Samantha shrugged, but kept silent.

"It's also one of the most horrific ways to die."

"I thought drowning wasn't meant to be so terrible," Amy said.

Gwyn nodded. "It isn't. I researched it for one of my novels."

"We're not talking about drowning. You know what we neglected to ask earlier? If the *intent* was to drown him. She had to hold him under water, but what if she wasn't trying to drown him, but instead make him drink?" Dr Engels said.

"Why would she have to render him unconscious to do that? She could've just poured him a glass of water," Amy said.

"Because he was severely, agonisingly afraid of water. I

should point out it wasn't something he was afraid of before coming to Perth, nor was it something he had any control over. The poor man contracted a virus, probably when he acquired one of those old scars Sam mentioned, another subtle clue."

Samantha nodded. "Go on. You may as well give the *denouement*."

"Not all of us speak Latin," Mug complained.

Gwyn laughed. "It's French."

"Yeah, well I learnt Spanish."

Dr Engels held up a hand. "Anyway, poor Pedro had *rabies*. That's why the couple were Mexican. They had to be from a country where the disease was present and well-known enough that they'd recognise what was occurring when he started to have symptoms."

"Why didn't they seek help?" Amy asked.

"I can think of a couple of reasons. They were in a foreign country and spoke little English. They might not have felt comfortable about it, or worried about the expense, plus, once symptoms show the disease is invariably fatal. They would have known he was doomed," Dr Engels said.

"But she smashed a bottle over his head," Amy protested.

"I don't think you understand how horrible this disease is," Samantha said. "The symptoms can start months or even years after a bite or scratch from an infected creature. If you know you've been infected you can take effective precautions, but if you don't, from the first symptoms appearing, it's a death sentence." Seeming to realise she was giving too much away, she nodded to Dr Engels to continue.

Dr Engels shuddered as he resumed his description. "And how. It starts mild and indistinct. You'd be hard-pressed to think it anything other than a cold. This can last for a couple of days. Then things go rapidly downhill. Remember, by this time its fatality is certain. You might get a tingling pain or itch near the original wound, but that is minor compared to the mental effects. There is an unrelenting sense of doom and fear. The person affected will ooze saliva non-stop. The regions in the victim's brain that produce rage become super-stimulated. Stop and imagine watching someone go through this. They would appear deranged. The victim becomes hypersensitive to sound, light and, well, pretty much everything. A mere breeze can cause convulsions. By this time there is an excruciatingly painful spasm of the muscles, but especially in the throat. Eventually, this seizure of the muscles will prevent them from breathing. But before that they will refuse all food and drink due to the intense pain consumption brings. They nearly always become hydrophobic, sorry, aquaphobic – deadly afraid of water, because they fear the idea of swallowing it. This compounds their rage. Death occurs within a couple of days from the first symptoms of a cold. Ramona must have known his symptoms were those of rabies. His raging and violence, as witnessed by the hotel staff, were symptoms of the disease. She knocked him unconscious in order to

174

get him to the bath to try to make him drink. In her mind it was the only way it could happen. He'd be forced to take in gulps of water. It might help with the seizures. She wasn't trying to drown him, just force him to drink. Though, drowning at that point would have been a mercy."

"Incredible," Brad said. "You know, I would let her go under those circumstances. Once there was a confirmed diagnosis of rabies, I wouldn't consider her actions to be homicide."

"And that would require?" Samantha prompted.

"An autopsy, which might take a couple of days to get the results. Especially considering the language barrier. It'd take time to work out what really happened." Brad smiled. "That's why there was the week's delay."

"Very neat," Gwyn said. "Would you mind if I used that as the basis for a story?"

"Not at all. Go right ahead."

"I thought you wrote romances," Amy said.

"The fact she stayed with him when the disease causes the victim to become furiously violent, not to mention witnessing his suffering, and putting herself in harm's way to tend to him as he died – Ramona must have loved him intensely. It's actually terribly romantic."

Mug grunted. "I say the law might not be as lenient as you think. Brad's opinion aside, and he's a good 'un, most cops would be too happy to get a slam dunk of a case like that. I mean an eyewitness, an abundance of evidence and a confession she had to do it."

Brad scowled. "No detective of mine would be allowed

to bring charges like that."

"But it's not always up to you is it?"

"No."

"So, I think my point is proven."

Amy nudged Brad. He grizzled but didn't say anything.

"Anyway, so how did I do?" Dr Engels asked.

"Right on nearly all counts," Samantha said.

"Nearly all?" The look of surprise was evident on Dr Engels' face.

"You were wrong about two things. There's a single case in the medical literature where someone who developed symptoms of rabies survived without prior vaccination," Samantha said. "And, secondly, we do have bat-born rabies in Australia. Unlike the Americas, ours is caused by a different but related virus called lyssavirus, and there have been three recorded deaths, all in the east."

"Well, none over here on the west of the country. I hope you'll overlook that tiny error and forgive my not being aware of them."

"Of course," Samantha said good-naturedly.

"I think that was an excellent first mystery for us. Any chance you'd like to become a regular?" Dr Engels asked.

"I thought you had your five."

"No reason why we can't have one more. Besides, in a few months we'll lose one or maybe even two of our group for a while," Dr Engels said with a grin in the direction of Amy and Brad.

"No way he's leaving me home with bubs by myself while he gets to come out and have fun," Amy said with a smirk. "Well, maybe if he makes it up to me."

Brad's phone buzzed loudly. A moment later, Samantha's phone did the same.

"Uh oh," they said together.

Brad read the message. "Um. It seems Yvette Malone has just been found dead in her bathtub at the Luxton."

"Drowned? We might have a reason why. Though why anyone would show her such mercy, I don't know," Gwyn said.

"What's your beef with our famous mining magnate? I thought she was meant to be all right."

"I have my reasons," Gwyn replied.

"Doc, I know the price of that champagne would cover my weekly mortgage, so thanks. The text was just to give us the heads up as Sam'll probably have to do the autopsy, and I'll have to support the investigation tomorrow, but I'd still better get going. It's going to be—"

Brad's phone rang. It was dispatch telling him to attend to the hotel as he was the nearest officer. Brad protested he was on his own. Dispatch's response reminded Brad of the level of surveillance he was given. He disconnected the call and turned to Samantha.

"Damn. They know we're both in the city and would like you to go with me to the body. Looks like we'll have to walk over the road."

Samantha nodded and together they said a quick goodbye. Brad immediately regretted drinking his and Amy's drinks. He hoped the short walk would clear his head.

A Billionaire's Bath

Brad and Samantha walked the short distance to the Luxton Hotel. Its large cream-coloured façade gave way to a beige interior. From the thick, plush carpets, to the leather chesterfield couches and armchairs adorning the foyer, the upmarket hotel was the epitome of old-school luxury. From experience, Brad knew that under the circumstances to go to the concierge desk rather than reception. Brad guessed his and Samantha's demeanour were what tipped off the concierge, who approached them the moment they were within earshot of her desk.

"You're the officials?" she asked. Brad appreciated the phrasing. Anyone overhearing wouldn't be alerted to a detective or medical examiner being in the hotel. Not that there were many people in the foyer at this time of the evening. Both Brad and Samantha nodded and were led to an express elevator, which serviced only the top five floors of the hotel. Brad wished the lighting was brighter. He'd had a few drinks before being summoned to the hotel, and they had added to his fatigue after a long day.

As they hurtled upwards, the concierge, Mary-Jane, told the detectives about Yvette Malone.

"She's stayed with us on and off for years. I'd say she's probably here for at least six or seven months a year."

"Why wouldn't she just buy an apartment in the city? I mean, she's a billionaire. Wouldn't that be cheaper?" Samantha said.

"Yes and no. I guess she gets to write it off to her company. Plus, with the way she orders room service, I'd say not having to pay a full-time cook or cleaner more than compensates. She also gets use of the business facilities of the hotel and conducts meetings here. It's probably cheaper and more convenient for her to live this way. No land tax, maintenance or rates. The way she also uses water, that's a good thing."

"What do you mean?" Brad asked.

"She practically lived in her spa bath. Our servers would deliver food to her while she was in there. It was usual for her to be in there for at least breakfast and dinner. Lunch would depend on whatever business meetings she had."

"That seems odd."

"I know. We only allowed four people to take her food. They were very well tipped and knew not to talk of what they saw."

"Such as?"

"That in the evenings Yvette would usually be in the spa with an eye mask and her Amar Sports headphones on. The jets would be going, and she wouldn't even notice the meal arrive, nor the plates being taken an hour or so later."

"Bizarre," Samantha said. "But they did talk though."

"Only to me. A big part of my role was to keep her happy. When what she pays covers two annual salaries, yet only requires an hour's labour per day, she's entitled to get away with being a bit odd."

"So, you're upset she's dead?" Brad asked.

"We're devastated. She was our favourite customer."

The elevator slowed and its doors opened.

"We're on the top floor?" Samantha queried.

"Yes. Yvette insisted on this particular room. The roof is just a roof, no rooftop bar or anything. This room has a balcony and spa jets in its bath. Yvette wanted both."

Mary-Jane led them down a long, straight corridor. She stopped at the last room on the right. Her card placed on the sensor turned the light on the lock from red to green.

A short, wardrobe-lined corridor opened into a large bedroom and living area. Brad was surprised the door to the bathroom opened to the main part of the room. He was used to them opening along the corridor.

The king-sized bed was tightly made. It appeared the room had been serviced and the bed not used between then and now. What was striking about the bed was the bright yellow bedsheets. Brad had stayed in the hotel early in his and Amy's relationship. Didn't they have beige sheets?

"What's with the bedding?" he asked.

"Oh that. Yvette's signature colour was sunflower yellow. She insisted her bedding and towels were that colour. Pretty smart too. As the only room with such a provision she could ensure they were only used by her. We even washed them separately."

"Why yellow?" Brad asked.

"Yellowcake. She owned a uranium mine. Why not make it a theme?" Samantha suggested.

"I should warn you it's not a pretty sight. The only thing I know has been done is that the jets were turned off. When the kitchen hand, Ben, came to retrieve the dining tray, she didn't acknowledge his presence, though that wasn't unusual, but then he saw the toaster and nearly tripped over the extension cord. Ben guessed she'd killed herself. He turned off the jets and power point, but you'll have to ask him why."

Mary-Jane pointed to the white cord plugged into a wall socket in the room. It snaked its way into the bathroom.

"So that has been—"

"Wait. The jets were on? I would've expected the power to go off," Brad said.

"It did. The short circuit occurred on the switch out here. The bathroom's power points are on a different circuit."

"Interesting," Samantha said.

"Yes, but let's see the body before we start theorising," Brad said quickly. Thankfully, Samantha took the hint and they each took a step towards the bathroom. Mary-Jane opened the door and let them past. What confronted them wasn't easy to see. The very overweight, naked body of Yvette Malone was lying in the bathtub. Under the water with her was a small white toaster. Hanging on the back of the door was a yellow, monogrammed bathrobe.

Brad was grateful for the bright light from the heat lamps. It forced his brain to switch off its melatonin production. Now if he could just get a coffee that would be great.

Steam rose off the bath water. "How long ago was she discovered?"

"About half an hour."

Brad tested the water. "That's still hot. If I had a bath that hot for as long as she does, I'd almost certainly faint when I got out."

"Oh yeah, your trigger-happy vagus nerve," Samantha said.

"Yep. Though more the resultant low blood pressure."

"The toaster's one of ours," Mary-Jane said.

"From this room?" Brad asked.

Mary-Jane shrugged. "I haven't looked."

Brad left the bathroom when Samantha began to examine the body. He returned a moment later. "There's another one in the cupboard. Why would she have two?"

"She had an appetite. Maybe she'd asked someone here for a second one?"

Brad shrugged.

"Take a look here," Samantha said, pointing to a scar on Yvette's chest. The inch-long mark was located about a centimetre below her collarbone and ran down the groove between the chest and shoulder.

"Looks surgical."

"Exactly. This is a D-type scar most likely from a pacemaker being inserted. For women they cut this way, rather than along the clavicle or collarbone, to make the scar less visible when wearing dresses. It also heals better that way due to different muscular tension on the skin. From the looks of the scar, she had the surgery at least six months ago. Maybe a year? It won't be hard to find out."

Brad felt that didn't match what he was seeing. "Can you arrange for the body to be taken to the morgue for an autopsy?"

Samantha nodded, unlocked her phone using face ID and asked the digital assistant to call Xing.

Brad slowly walked around the small bathroom, carefully examining the splashes of water around the room and taking photos of what interested him. He then went to the main room and repeated the action, before stepping out onto the balcony. While there he took a few more photos on his phone.

When he returned to the bathroom Samantha said, "Xing will collect the body with Ally in half an hour or so. They're just finishing a transfer from Royal Perth."

"Thanks, Sam. Mary-Jane, will you greet them when they get here?"

"Sure."

"Good. By the way you don't have to stay here with us. We'll just do our thing until they get here."

"You want me to leave?"

"More a case of I don't want to keep you from your job. We can handle this. Would you please ask the food server to wait in one of your meeting rooms or staff lounge. We'll see them soon."

"Uh, I can't do that. I sent Ben home."

"Why?" Brad asked.

"He'd seen something traumatic. I didn't want him to remain here or let slip what he'd seen to other staff."

That was a small mercy. Delaying the interview to the next morning would mean Brad could sleep off his fatigue before then. He was potentially missing things because of his tiredness.

He walked Mary-Jane to the door, and when she had left, he used his phone to take a video of the scene from the hallway, to the bathroom, to living area and the balcony. The balcony had cream painted concrete to thigh height, then two parallel wires before the black cylindrical balustrade. The balcony was separated by about a metre gap from the one next door. As such it was relatively private. The view over the Swan River to South Perth was spectacular. Brad stuck his head over the railing and looked up. There was a large section of wall before he could see an edge indicating the top of the building. To his right as he faced the water was another balcony. To his left was more wall before the corner of the building.

Brad returned to help Samantha finish the bagging and tagging of items from the room. There was a sample of the bathwater, hair and fibre samples from the bathmat, carpet and bedding, and the toaster and extension cord. The toaster's wires were exposed near where the cord entered the toaster. The wires were not frayed, though. When the water had drained from the bath, they collected more hair samples, which had caught in the drain. Brad also noted the drainpipe in the bath was made from copper. That was important. It would give the electricity a path to follow and mean it would take longer to activate a circuit breaker.

"So, what do you think? Is it suicide or murder?" Samantha asked.

"Given the one power point in here is still in use and her toothbrush is still plugged in, I'd theorise it's not suicide. The normal behaviour would be to plug the toaster into the nearest power point, the one by the sink. Only, since that switch has extra protection on it, it wouldn't work. So, if that was where you started then wouldn't you unplug it and try the power point in the living area. But in that scenario, you wouldn't plug back in what you'd unplugged because you wouldn't be intending to use it again. The water on the floor doesn't support such a proposition."

"What do you mean?"

"There wasn't any. The floor wasn't wet, so she hadn't gone into the bath then walked over to change where the toaster was plugged. She hadn't dropped the toaster in while standing either. If she had, she'd have fallen into the bath, and well, uh, she's a large person. That would have caused a lot of splashes. But that also supports why I think she was murdered."

"Huh?" Samantha grunted.

"No big splashes. She was clearly lying down when the toaster was put in the bath. That doesn't make sense.

You'd at least be sitting upright, wouldn't you?"

"I haven't thought about it."

"I hadn't before either. But I just can't see someone who is suiciding slipping into the bath, lying down while holding up the toaster, then gently placing it in the water. I feel confident this is murder."

"I'm inclined to agree. Whoever did it must've known her habit."

"But didn't Mary-Jane say Yvette wore a mask and Amar brand earphones? Where are they? They're not in the bedroom, which is why I'm beginning to think someone did kill her. I'd guess the killer took them. It was planned. I mean they brought an extension cord and hotel toaster. Maybe there was a knock at the door from Ben coming to collect dishes or something interrupted them after they dropped it in the bath. They had to get out. They grabbed the mask and earphones because it wouldn't make sense to wear them in a suicide, but the killer ran out of time to take the second toaster from the room. In a way that's a good thing as it speaks to pre-meditation, which means it's definitely a murder charge."

Samantha nodded. "I'm inclined to agree. The fact she had a pacemaker meant that even if the shock was short, it would likely kill her. 'Course I could be wrong. The scar could be from surgery to her shoulder."

"But where would the killer go? If they were interrupted by a knock at the door, they couldn't exactly go out that way."

"True. What about the balcony? Maybe they jumped to

the next one and went through that room?"

"Then all we have to do is find out who was in that room. That should be easy enough," Brad said.

"We should be able to get video of them too. That could be good. I'm so tired though," Brad said. "I wish it could all wait until tomorrow."

"You mean later today. We crossed over half an hour ago."

"I'm so tired," Brad repeated.

"You shouldn't have tried to hide Amy's news by drinking her drinks."

"Agreed. That was a mistake. Especially with that room of people."

"We're about done here in terms of an investigation. Go home. Get some sleep. We'll reconvene in the morning. I'd like to be there when you interview Ben if I can. There are some things I'd like to hear from him."

"Let's make it for 11.00 am then?"

"Done."

"I'll get Ben's info from Mary-Jane on my way out."

"I'll stick around until Xing and Ally get here. They shouldn't be much longer."

They gathered their things and did a final sweep of the room. Samantha sat on the bed and started playing on her phone. "I'll be fine. You go."

Brad almost walked straight into Xing and Ally as he opened the door leave.

"They're here," Brad called.

"Don't wait. I'll help them. You go."

Brad fell asleep almost as soon as his head hit the pillow. Later that morning, feeling a lot more refreshed, he was keen to take another look at the case. Once in his office, he took out his phone and transferred all the images and videos from the case to his computer. He watched as each image appeared in thumbnail in the folder. The absence of the eye mask and Amar earphones convinced Brad it was a murder. But why would someone murder Yvette? Sure, no one got to be a billionaire without stepping on a few toes, but this seemed like a professional hit rather than someone scorned. It was good that the death hadn't been announced yet, though surely when her staff couldn't reach her the alarm would soon be raised. Brad estimated he'd have up to an hour before the news began to leak into the community.

Brad typed Yvette's name into a search engine. The first tab was a list of profiles and fluff pieces from the media. Brad clicked on the 'news' tab. The third article caught his attention. It said Yvette was refusing to yield to a hostile take-over bid for her mining company from none other than Athol Fugate. Brad tried not to scowl at the name. He'd been trying to arrest Athol for years. The man seemed to be involved in more criminal enterprises than legal ones.

It appeared Athol had acquired enough shares to force his way on to the board of the company through controlling a voting block. He then continued to try acquiring more shares with a view to being able to gain more board seats. Yvette had realised what was up and implemented a counter-attack. First, she'd put in place a golden parachute for her executives and herself. The article compared this to Meg Whitman, the former CEO of Hewlett-Packard, who stood to receive almost $91 million if there was a change of control at the company, and more than $51 million if her employment was terminated. The speculation about a hostile take-over had driven the share price up as the process usually involved an offer above the market price of shares as an incentive for shareholders to sell. Easy profit could be made if the take-over came to fruition.

Realising the shares were becoming worth more than Athol could afford to pay, the article mentioned Yvette had concocted a secondary Pac-Man defence. This technique was simple. Athol's pursuit of her company had led his to become vulnerable to the same strategy he was employing against Yvette. He couldn't afford to increase his shareholding in his own company, so Yvette had started buying the available shares. She had soon amassed enough shares that it was expected she would be able to force her way on to its board at its next meeting. In Pac-Man terms Athol was the ghost attacking her, but his over-expenditure was the power-pill needed to transform Yvette's Pac-Man from pursued to pursuer. Brad grinned when he read Athol was at risk of losing some control over his company because of his own greed. It served him right.

If Athol was involved, and it was an 'if', then Brad would have to tread carefully. The one time he'd come close to arresting Athol a patsy had confessed and taken the fall.

Brad's chair creaked as he lent back and put his feet on his desk. He found it mentally freeing to spread out in his tiny office. It was as though as he spread out his body, his mind uncramped and could expand its thinking.

A vibration alerted Brad to a message from Samantha to say she was arriving at the station.

~

Brad greeted Samantha warmly. He was surprised at how fresh she looked compared to his still tired state.

"How is it you look like you've just had ten hours sleep?"

"I've only had four. But I live alone and have a good routine. My body has forgiven me for one night's indiscretion. Don't worry, if tonight's bad, I'll look like you tomorrow."

"I somehow doubt that."

Samantha laughed. "Well, there is the make-up too. By the way there's news. The bath water contained urine, which makes sense given she practically lived in the bath. That increases the risk of death by electrocution. Also, I put a few of the hair follicles we collected through an ELISA test for drug use. It's come back positive, so Steve's going to run a GC/MS and get more specific results. That will take a day or maybe two, but I thought it might help us with a starting point. It could be a drug deal gone wrong."

"That's a very different theory to what I've come up with this morning." Brad explained Yvette's connection to

Athol Fugate.

"So, two competing ideas. That's good," Samantha said.

"Exactly. We can put forward each as a hypothesis and test whether the evidence supports the idea."

"The scientific method strikes again."

They both laughed.

"But seriously, how are we going to prove one or the other?" Samantha asked.

"Let's go interview Ben. He discovered her. Maybe he'll let us know something we missed. I mean, we were both a bit tired when we got there. I'll also get the concierge to come in tomorrow afternoon, once your results are back. There's more going on there, but I can't figure out what."

They spent a few minutes sorting out a list of questions to ask Ben. What Brad really wanted to hear was his description of what he saw and heard from the moment he knocked on the hotel room door.

~

"I knocked on the door," Ben began.

He was sitting opposite Brad and Samantha in the interview room, a steaming coffee on the table in front of him. Brad had been aghast when Ben had asked for it to be microwaved after being poured. He'd explain he was used to sipping a coffee over at least an hour and liked it *hot*.

"I paused as I always do. Most of the time there's no response from Ms Malone, but we're under instruction to wait for thirty seconds, then take the food in regardless.

Nine times out of ten she's in the bath with her headphones and eye mask on and totally oblivious. I wheel the trolley next to the bath and leave it there."

"And what happens on the tenth time?" Brad asked.

"Then, she's up and doing something like watching the news."

"Have you noticed a pattern to those occasions? Like is it a particular day of the week, or time of month?"

Ben thought about the question. "I'd guess it's more common in the last week of the month, just before she goes away for a couple of nights."

Brad wrote the words 'stops before board meeting' on his pad and showed Samantha, who nodded.

"What was she like?" Brad asked.

"We didn't exactly talk much. I didn't hang around while Ms Malone was in the bath. It wasn't a pretty sight, if that's okay to say. When she was up, she wasn't chatty. It was just a courteous thank you or comment on her going away. But if you want to know what she was like you should ask MJ, Mary-Jane."

"Why do you say that?" Brad asked.

"They were pretty close. I'd see them talking a bit. One time, I even saw her give MJ what look like at least a thousand dollars in cash."

"Was she generous with tips?"

"Ms Malone wasn't the warmest person, but she knew how to keep us onside by paying. There was always a twenty dollar note on the floor near the door for us when we delivered food. That was cool. It was a nice bonus for the easiest of jobs."

"So, you didn't want to see her dead?"

"No. She was awesome. I made an extra hundred bucks a week from her. Sometimes more. All four of the chosen few, that's what we called her servers, made that. We loved when she stayed. MJ too. She seemed nicer when Ms Malone was with us."

Brad switched to his messiest handwriting in case Ben glimpsed the page. He wrote, 'did MJ know about the drug use?'

"What do you think Yvette, sorry, Ms Malone, was doing in the bath so much?" Samantha asked.

"Blissing out. I mean it seemed almost meditative. She was totes unaware of her surroundings when she was in there. I always assumed she was meditating. Either that or trying to cook the weight off. I mean that bath was always steaming."

"Do you have any further questions, Sam?" Brad asked.

"Just one. Did Ms Malone ever vomit?"

Ben jumped. "How'd you know that? Sometimes, yes. A few times when she used the business rooms. I wondered if she was really sick and that's why she would go away, to get treatment."

Brad thanked Ben for coming and answering their questions. He led him through the maze of corridors out of the station, then made a beeline back to the interview room, where Samantha was writing on her notepad.

"Sam, what was the deal with that last question? It seems like you have an idea about something."

194

"I think I know why she lived in the bath. I'll need the results of the autopsy today, and hair follicle analysis tomorrow to confirm."

Brad stared at her, then made circles with his hand. "Well? What's the reason?"

"You have to keep this theory between us, but I think she was a stoner."

"What? How? She ran a billion-dollar company."

"You always tell me you follow the wear patterns of things to work out the regular behaviour of people. In this case I'm following the behaviour to work out the wear pattern."

"What wear pattern?"

"The erosion on her teeth. I noticed it when her mouth opened when Xing, Ally and me lifted her out the bath."

"If it was revealed she was a drug user it could be damaging for her. Why go to a hotel where it might be obvious?"

"Actually, I think it may be the most logical place for her. If I'm right, she needed to be able to not leave the bath. Room service, cleaners, proximity to the bath for after business meetings, it all fits. There's more discretion in hotels than from personal employees."

"What's the bath got to do with it?"

"There was a case in a medical journal I read a while back. A young woman was admitted to hospital for the fifth time for … uh … what in layman's terms is regular vomiting. The only thing which alleviated her nausea was a hot shower or bath. The hotter the better. It took the attending doctor a lot of work to figure out she was a chronic marijuana smoker. Her habit had led to a rare condition called cannabinoid hyperemesis. Emesis means vomiting."

"And I can figure out the rest. Got it."

"The patient didn't believe the doctor, though her condition improved the longer she was in hospital. In fact, that's why she improved; she couldn't smoke while she was there. It would take a few weeks after she left the hospital before the symptoms returned, so the patient wouldn't accept it was the marijuana. But the hot water gave relief. That's why Yvette 'lived' in the bath."

"And why she wore the mask and earphones. She was enjoying the high."

"But the room didn't smell of smoke."

"The balcony," they said together.

Brad asked Samantha to follow him to his office, where he opened his laptop and brought up the video he'd recorded the night before.

"I recorded this because I was so tired. I knew I wasn't catching everything I should, so I took a long video of the room."

Brad fast-forwarded until he reached him opening the sliding door to the balcony. The picture quality deteriorated a little as the balcony was only illuminated from the lights in the main room, though all of them were turned on.

When the camera panned to the easternmost corner Brad paused. "There," he said, pointing to a shallow hole in the concrete. "I bet she squats or sits on the balcony and smokes her joint, then stubs the joints out there on the wall—"

"Not a bong?"

"We didn't find one, so no. She must have known it's easier to hide the evidence when you smoke a joint versus a bong. If we go back, we might get lucky and find some ash. It hasn't rained since last night, so it's possible."

"So, she'd stub them out in that pit, because if you were sitting on the ground it would seem like a super-mini ashtray, then what, toss the butt over the balcony?"

"They're actually called bugholes, even though they're caused by air bubbles."

Samantha raised an eyebrow.

"My sister was a structural engineer. She used to complain that the regulations for buildings didn't limit the number of bugholes, only their size. Given they weakened the concrete she felt it was an oversight. But yes, I think what you said is exactly what she'd have done."

"How did she get the drugs?" Samantha asked.

Brad grinned. "Who was the only person she seemed friendly with?"

"The concierge, Mary-Jane," they said in unison.

"So, the thousand dollars wasn't just a tip," Samantha said.

"Who'd leave a thousand-dollar tip?"

Samantha shrugged nonchalantly.

"What? You would?"

"I earn nearly half a mill' a year and live in a two-bed

apartment. I have a lot of savings. Maybe not that high, but if I'd stayed in place that long, then maybe."

Brad groaned. "I so got into the wrong line of work."

"Only if money is your motivator. You're a good cop and in the right place. But if you ever need a loan…" Sam said with a smile.

"Let's just go get MJ shall we? What about the lab result?"

"I'll get Steve to look for marijuana, rather than the full spectrum. That should speed up the testing. Let's go get a morning tea slash very early lunch. Then I'll do the autopsy, and you can arrange for MJ to visit this afternoon instead of tomorrow and go look at the balcony again. We should have the hair and autopsy results by the time I see you again."

~

Brad was grateful he'd had two coffees with his meal. Combined with the excitement of the case, the caffeine was making him feel perky. Steve, the junior ME, had messaged to say the hair sample was positive for chronic marijuana use, and Samantha had called to say the internals examined in the autopsy matched the symptoms of cannabinoid hyperemesis and chronic marijuana use. "The hair test gave me an indication of how regularly she's used over the last ninety days. Let's just say it was a lot," Samantha said. "The autopsy confirmed the cause of death was electrocution, with the pacemaker and underlying pathology making Yvette particularly susceptible to that manner of death."

Brad reviewed the surveillance tapes from the hotel for the previous week. There were two cameras: one pointed from the end of the hallway next to Yvette's room, back towards the elevators, and one which ran the other way. After half an hour of viewing the footage, the only thing that surprised Brad was the amount of food Yvette ordered, particularly in the evenings. She must have had the munchies really badly. Brad noticed MJ visit every second day. She would stay for about ten minutes each time. It was odd given all the other deliveries seemed to last as short as possible. Maybe they really did have a bit of a friendship happening. Brad slowed down the playback when he finally reached the rough time of the murder. Ben wheeled his trolley to the door, knocked and waited. The timer on the screen matched the thirty seconds Ben said he'd waited. Ben even seemed to note the time on his phone to make sure he waited long enough. An hour later Ben returned to collect the dishes. Again, he waited thirty seconds before entering. Brad sighed. That thirty seconds was probably how the murderer got away. They could have waited behind a curtain or on the balcony for the body to be discovered. When Ben ran out the room, they would have left. Brad waited and watched. Sure enough, a minute later Ben ran out the room and towards the elevators. A few seconds later, Brad was surprised to see a figure emerge, not from Yvette's room, but the room next door. It was a short man who moved like he was in good physical condition, but Brad couldn't get a good angle on his face. He quickly switched to the second camera and was relieved when a full-frontal image of the man's face could be seen, particularly as he got closer to the elevators. The resolution was good enough that they might get a hit from the facial recognition software. Brad was going to phone the hotel and ask them to send over all details, including receipts from the occupant of that room, when he decided to drive over and ask in person. That way he could also get a second look at that balcony. It would be easier to meet MJ there too.

~

Brad had run his errands at the hotel and had a chat with Ben, when it was time to interview Mary-Jane who arrived promptly at 3.00 pm. She was wearing a flattering, lemon-coloured woollen jumper and black knee length skirt. In contrast to the evening before, she also appeared nervous.

"Mary-Jane," Brad began.

"Call me MJ."

"MJ," Samantha interjected. "As I mentioned last night, I'm the city's medical examiner. I've confirmed that Yvette died from electrocution. It didn't help she had a pacemaker, which short circuited as well."

"Okay," MJ said slowly.

"But I think you know there may be other factors involved in her death."

"What d-do you mean?" MJ stammered.

"We know she was smoking marijuana every day," Brad said. "I found some ash on her balcony in the bugholes of the concrete. I also found a couple of butts from the joints on the ground below. They're a match."

Brad paused. He was lying about the match as the test wasn't yet complete, though he reasoned it was highly likely to be an accurate assumption. MJ didn't seem like the type to question it.

"We carefully sounded out Ben about what he knew about drugs in the hotel. He wasn't aware of any, and I have no reason to believe he was lying. Which means they weren't rampant, nor were lots of deals being done."

"Absolutely not," MJ said.

"However, I wonder if your employer knew you were supplying Yvette with marijuana?" Brad said as casually as possible. It was a leading question. A yes or no would be an admittance of guilt. The only correct response was to question the assumption of the question and say she'd never dealt drugs anywhere. Whether by mental slip or lack of thinking through the question, MJ fell into the trap.

"No, they didn't know," she said. It was clear MJ had assumed the police knew she was the dealer.

"But that's why Ben saw Yvette paying you a thousand dollars?"

"Yes."

"And Yvette was the only person you supplied to?"

"Yes."

"You can help yourself if you let us know your supplier."

"What if they get upset I've dobbed on them?"

"They won't know. I'll say we were aware of a threat on Ms Malone's life so were watching the hotel. We realised you were supplying her with drugs so followed you and observed an exchange, so started following them. Personal use is not illegal, but large-scale supply is. But equally, unless they're involved in something more serious, we won't be pressing charges against them. We'd try to get them to give us information on the hard-drug supply. That's our real target. If they're uncooperative, then yes, we'll press charges."

"But you won't be suspected as the source," Samantha said.

Brad appreciated Sam's understanding of how her subtle reinforcement would shape MJ's opinion of the offer.

"Fine. The supplier is a guy named Hink Brynck. I'm not sure if Hink is his real first name, but that's what he's called. He operates from London Court. Look for a guy wearing white shoes, black shorts or pants, a white shirt or jumper and a black fedora hat. Ask him for directions to the WACA, WAPA campus in Burswood."

"That's the most convoluted conjunction of places in the city I've ever heard," Brad said.

"Exactly, that's how he knows you're cool. He'll walk with you to the corner and sell you a map, which will contain the pot."

"How much?"

"Two hundred will get you nine grams of the good stuff, a legal amount for personal use."

"Thank you," Brad said. After confirming Yvette's bath habits with MJ, he let her go with a warning.

~

202

Brad followed MJ's procedure the next morning. It had been easy to spot Hink. He'd walked with Brad to where the misnamed London Court met St George's Terrace where Detective Sally Summers was waiting in an unmarked car. Brad completed the transaction and established what he had looked like marijuana. Speaking softly, he said, "Thanks, Hink. How about you get into the car with that other detective and me, and we go and have a little chat?" Brad discretely showed Hink his badge. "I'm sure we'd both prefer if there wasn't a scene."

Hink scowled but got into the backseat of the car, followed by Brad. Normally, Brad would sit in the front or be driving, but Brad felt maintaining the flow was important. Hink sat in silence, so Brad started talking to his colleague.

"Did you hear that Yvette's daughter is going to inherit nearly all of her mother's estate, bar a hundred million going to set up a scholarship in her name at the University of Western Australia?" Brad said. A university spokesperson had made the announcement, apparently in accordance with the conditions of the will. Brad suspected it was a way for Yvette to control the narrative about herself after her death. He glanced at Hink and noticed him twitch when Yvette's name was spoken. What did he know?

"That girl just became ri-ich," Sally said, briefly turning to face the men in the back.

"She's not the only one," Brad replied.

"What?" Sally asked, glancing from the road to Brad

and back.

"I just found out how much MEs earn. It's between four and five hundred k."

"Really? Wow."

"Anyway, next round is on Sam."

"Cool. Though in her defence she did spend over a decade at uni, has medical and pathological qualifications and spends a lot of time cutting up bodies. It's not pleasant work," Sally said.

"You have a point. I couldn't do it."

For the rest of the short journey, Brad and Sally traded a couple of 'war stories' from their days at the police academy. Hink listened intently and seemed to relax the more they left him alone.

~

Once in the interview room, Brad and Sally sat opposite Hink. A slight bead of sweat appeared on his forehead. Good. The freshly stimulated nerves associated with the interrogation meant he could be bargained with. Brad went through his prepared story of how they'd been following up a threat to Ms Malone and realised Hink was the source of her supply of drugs. Hink nodded occasionally throughout the story. It was clear he'd heard about Yvette's death, which had been splashed all over the news.

"Unfortunately, we were unable to stop her from being killed," Brad said. He lowered his voice. "And that makes us look bad. Do you know what makes us look good?"

"Arrests," Hink said.

"Especially for drugs. It means we can say things like

we're cleaning up the streets. Perhaps you can help us with that? We know you only deal with pot, which isn't so interesting to us. Perhaps you know of people or groups who deal with harder stuff?"

Hink's expression changed to resignation, then a curious twitch appeared at the edges of his mouth. Was that a wry smile?

"You admit people dying on your watch makes you look bad, and I don't want to give up my one friend who dabbles with cocaine, so what if I give you something better?"

"Like what?"

"I know who murdered Ms Malone. Or rather, I know where they are."

"Who?"

"I don't know their real name. He's just called the I.M.Phreak. That's I dot M and freak with a 'ph'. It's both 'I'm Phreak' and Imp reak 'cos he takes risks to get to someone that others wouldn't. But he's also imp like."

Brad's mind raced. He was near certain the killer had jumped from their balcony to Yvette's and back again. Hink's description fit their suspect.

"Could you recognise him?"

"Sure. But let's be clear. At this stage you haven't charged me, nor given me reason to call a lawyer. I'd like something in writing to confirm my giving you this information means I won't be charged for dealing pot."

"Sure. Tell you what. I'll get our sketch artist to come in and work with you to create an image of I.M.Phreak.

Meanwhile, I'll get an agreement drawn up and arrange a photo line-up. If everything matches and we catch him, you're a free man."

~

The sketch matched the photo from the surveillance camera and Hink identified the correct photo easily. When the deal was signed, he'd let the detectives know their target was someone he sold to, who had implied exactly how Yvette had died before her death had been announced. Their target had apparently told Hink to let him know if he ever needed to get someone 'outta da way'.

The identity software had matched his photo to a drivers licence. His real name was Robert Allain. Now the detectives were outside the school where Robert worked as a P.E. and science teacher. They had identified his car via its licence plate and knew he was still at the school. A bell had rung and a wave of students were now streaming out of the school.

"P.E. Huh. What if he runs?" Sally asked.

"I guess we chase. Good thing I run all those laps of the lake each week."

"Let's pretend we're parents of a student."

"Good idea. Remember to call him Mr Allain like a student would with their parent."

They waited another ten minutes, by which time the wave of students had slowed to a trickle and finally stopped. They exited the car and walked towards the teacher car park as they noticed a few teachers beginning to leave. They kept close together like parents would, walking as slowly as they could manage without making it too obvious they were stalling.

Sally nudged Brad and broke into a stride. She raised her hand and waved. "Mr Allain," she called.

Robert looked at them questioningly. His face didn't register any recognition of them. As they got closer, Sally again called out, "We'd like to talk to you about our kid."

Robert twitched. Brad realised what mistake he'd picked up on. A parent would more typically say their child's name or son or daughter, not kid.

"Who's your kid?" Robert asked. His deep voice didn't seem to match his wiry and diminutive body.

"Sophie," Brad said. Unfortunately, at the same time Sally said, "Ashley."

Robert turned and ran parallel to the detectives. He was heading for the side gate of the school.

Brad sighed and started his pursuit. Keeping a visual would be important as Robert probably knew shortcuts to wherever he was heading. Brad needed to run fast but not go into a flat out sprint. If he sprinted, in under a minute he'd use up all his short-term, creatine-fuel and conk out. Robert was in good shape and it took a few minutes before Brad heard Sally catch up to them in the police car, its siren blaring.

Robert kept glancing back to see if Brad was still pursuing. Where was he trying to get to? This was a suburban street, but there was a train station nearby. That could be an easy place to lose a tail. They weaved between school children and a couple of dogs being walked to collect the kids from school, but mostly the street was quiet.

It wasn't the cliché of a kid running out to chase a ball, a car door opening, nor a glance back and run into a pole which caused Robert to stumble and fall, rather it was a basketball. Two girls were playing one-on-one basketball in their driveway. A long- range shot hit the rim and the ball flew back past the players and into Robert's path. Brad watched it unfold as though in slow motion. Robert gave another look over his shoulder toward Brad and didn't see the ball, but when his front foot landed on it, he fell, badly twisting his ankle. Robert cried out in pain.

Brad jogged up. "Robert Allain," he said between puffed breaths. "You're under arrest."

He took out his handcuffs and placed them over Robert's wrists. Sally turned off the siren as she pulled up. She'd seen the fall and brought a first aid kit with her.

Brad activated the instant icepack and strapped it to Robert's ankle with a long non-stick bandage. He then helped him into the unmarked police car.

"You'll note we're treating you well," Brad said as Sally started the drive to the station.

Robert grunted. Brad tried not to smile. An angry person could be turned through redirecting their anger onto someone else. Would that person be Athol Fugate? That would be ideal if that was how this case worked out.

Brad made eye contact with Robert and held it as he asked, "I take it Athol Fugate put you up to murdering Ms Malone?"

Robert nodded.

Brad started daydreaming about slapping a pair of handcuffs on Athol; it would be so satisfying. While Brad was in his reverie, and despite having his hands in cuffs behind his back, Robert was able to manipulate a phone out of his pocket. Brad only realised Robert had received a message when it was too late. The image on Robert's phone was of a woman, who Brad guessed was in her seventies. Robert's gasp told Brad all he needed to know about who the photo was and who it was from. Athol must have had someone watching Robert as a precaution.

~

Robert readily confessed to the murder. He'd taken the room next to Yvette's over the last week and had noticed her routine of smoking a joint or two on the balcony in the evenings, then running the spa for hours. The soft rumble of the jets was audible in his room. He tested his chosen method of execution in his room using a stray cat he had trapped and snuck into his room in a bag. He'd already bought an extension cord as the bath was further away from the sink than the toaster cord could reach.

"The cat had enough room to keep its head above water, though I did have to put a weighted washing basket over it. When I dropped the toaster in there was a click at the wall and the cat was still trying to get out. That was when I noticed the RCD light on the switch was activated. It didn't take much to find the reset for it, but in hunting for it, I noticed the wall switches in the room were different, so I tried one of those. This time the cat … uh

… went silent. It's an old building, I guess there isn't much of an RCD on those circuits."

Brad winced. The poor cat.

"I shouldn't have looked down before I jumped to her balcony. It may have only been a metre and easily achievable, but missing would have meant death."

Making it also meant that, Brad thought to himself.

"It was tricky as I had to jump with the toaster and extension cord. Once I was in the room it didn't take a moment to drop it in the bath with her. She was so zonked and with that mask and music, I doubt she ever knew I was there."

"And then?" Brad asked.

"I heard someone knock at the door. I knew I wouldn't have much time. I took the mask and earphones, as they didn't seem right for the suicide I was trying to stage. I bolted to the balcony and jumped back without thinking. It was only later I realised I forgot to get her toaster, but I couldn't go back as the body had been discovered and there was too much risk of getting caught, so I left. I'd paid with a prepaid gift credit card and used a fake name so couldn't be tracked that way. I noticed the camera at the end of the hall, so made sure I turned away from it as I left."

"There was another one by the elevators," Brad said.

"Dammit. So that's how."

"What happened to the cat?"

"I chucked it off the balcony. It was night. I checked it wasn't going to hit anyone."

Brad hadn't seen it when he had searched for the joint butts. He guessed someone had disposed of it.

"And Athol Fugate was the one who hired you?" Brad queried.

"No, I don't know who that is," Robert said. His face betrayed the lie, but Brad knew he was helpless to get Robert to admit it. Brad cursed himself for not patting Robert down before putting him in the car, but he was so puffed and mentally tired he hadn't been thinking straight. The photo, Brad guessed, was of Robert's mother. A clear threat that bad things would happen to her if Robert talked.

Brad wished Sally had seen Robert's nod confirming Athol had hired him to murder Ms Malone, but she'd been focused on the road. It wouldn't have mattered anyway. Even if he'd said yes aloud, without a sworn statement it would hold no weight in court. The knowledge he couldn't get to Athol because of his own action, or inaction, was frustrating. Brad was so angry with himself he slammed his fists on the table.

Robert jumped, but appeared to stay calm.

"So, who put you up to it?" Brad asked. An icy tone had crept into his voice.

"I don't know what you mean. This was my idea," Robert said with a face that betrayed his guile.

"Bullshit," Brad said.

"No, true shit," Robert replied.

Brad clenched his fist, and stood angrily. "You *will* go to jail. I hope it's not easy for you."

He left the room, shutting the door with more force than he intended. Athol had gotten away again. Brad was determined to get him for a crime of his one day.

The Hartog Tulip

The morning news presenter outdid themself with a gushing announcement as simple as it was surprising; a man who owned no diamond mines, declared a mine of his had found the world's first orange diamond. The presenter was unequivocal; it was not a cognac, champagne or yellow gem, but a pure orange. They went on to say that the stone was 12.77 carats, just larger than the Argyle Pink Jubilee, the largest pink diamond found at Western Australia's Argyle diamond mine.

The presenter said the owner was Athol Fugate. Brad grimaced. He'd had several run-ins with Athol in the past, and each time Athol had escaped conviction for the crime Brad was investigating.

Brad followed up by reading an article on the find in his newspaper. He still preferred to get a printed copy delivered each morning. The stone was to be called the Hartog Tulip since it was found near where the Dutch explorer Dirk Hartog had landed in Shark Bay in 1616. Given the price of Argyle pink diamonds being about a million dollars a carat in larger stones, the insurance value of the stone, when cut to its final state of about eight carats, was estimated to be nine million dollars. There was an irony to the price; the salt mine where it was found only had an annual turnover of that amount.

Given Athol's involvement, Brad was immediately suspicious of the find. A new type of diamond from a salt mine? He phoned his mentor and friend, Dr Engels. It was easier to ask him than a technical search of literature. The doctor was an early riser and often messaged before 7.00 am, so Brad knew he would be up for a call.

"Greetings Doc, have you read the paper today or seen the news?"

"Of course," Dr Engels said with his usual warmth.

"Did you read about the Hartog Tulip?"

"A load of twaddle. Totally the wrong type of ground to extract diamonds from."

"Thank you, that was my thought too, but could it be real, just found somewhere else?"

"Yes. Though it's not my area, so I guess I could be wrong and it could be found there. Sometimes colour in diamonds is due to a slight contamination of the carbon with other elements, but for others it's just the crystalline arrangement. My understanding from one of the articles I read is that it has been certified by the Diamond Grading Laboratory of Australia. It's very possible it's real."

"And the potential outcome if it were real?"

"It might boost the value of the mine for a sale or just boost the share price, though I doubt any serious investor would be fooled."

Brad's felt the anger rise within him. "That's the thing. It's the 'mum and dad' investors who'd get hurt in such a scam, those who can least afford it."

"You're right. They're revealing the final cut of the gem to the world in six months at the finale of the fundraising for His Majesty's Theatre. There will be a gala and a performance by some of our best opera singers. That's why it's on the news today, to coincide with the fundraising launch."

"I haven't heard about that."

"I've been sent an invitation," Dr Engels said matter-of-factly.

"Oh."

"Such things aren't usually my cup of tea, but because I sponsor things here and there, I get sent invitations frequently."

"Are you going?"

"I was considering it. I've been seeing someone, and he's into the arts, so I was thinking of asking if he wanted to attend."

"You haven't asked him yet? What's holding you back?"

"It's six months away."

"So?"

"His idea of a good evening is to go somewhere loud and be seen, or to go to a show."

"Which isn't yours."

"No. Fireside chats are more my thing, which is why

I'm not sure it's going to work out."

"You've given me a lot of great advice, so let me give you some for a change."

Dr Engels laughed in a way which seemed supportive of the idea. "Sure."

"What if the differences between you are the opportunity for each of you to grow? And in that growth, grow together and form a lasting bond?"

"I think the student has become the master. Okay. I'll give it more of a go, but if it doesn't work out, how about you be my plus one for the gala?"

"Deal."

~

Five and a half months later

A summons to the morgue within the Royal Perth Hospital led to Brad finding himself staring at the body of a middle-aged man named Jacob. Jacob was lying on a gurney freshly wheeled in from an ambulance. He'd been struck once by a bouncer, Nikau, at the casino. The incident had been caught by the venue's security cameras. The footage had already been shared with the police and clearly showed Jacob being escorted out of the venue by two security staff and being let go. As the security staff returned inside, they said something to Nikau and pointed to Jacob. An interview with the security staff revealed Jacob had harassed several of the younger female staff in the casino and groped one employee when she refused to serve him another drink. In Jacob's words, if she wasn't going to get him a drink, perhaps she could satisfy his needs another way.

After stumbling about for a few moments Jacob tried to re-enter the casino. Nikau, a very large, muscular man, looked unconcerned by Jacob in the footage. Nikau held him back by simply placing his right hand on Jacob's chest. Nikau looked bored by the encounter. With his size and reach advantage, Jacob couldn't hit him, despite several swings at Nikau' face. Then Jacob did something stupid. He kicked Nikau in the groin. Instinctively, Nikau punched Jacob with his left hand. Both crumpled to the ground. Only one got back up.

~

Jacob had died en route to the hospital, and Brad had been summoned by dispatch to investigate the matter. The issue was what constituted an 'equal force' reply to being kicked in the groin, and how this fit in with the state's One-Punch Law. If the force was deemed excessive, despite being a single strike, and the victim died as a direct or indirect result of the assault, then Nikau was guilty of a crime. This was true, even if the bouncer didn't intend or foresee Jacob's death. The maximum penalty for the crime was ten years in prison. There was the possible defence of provocation. Nikau's response was clearly instinctive, and he'd already showed much restraint by simply holding Jacob back. What would determine the outcome for the bouncer would be the cause of death and determination of Nikau's state of mind during the incident.

~

Brad had interviewed Nikau at the casino. It had been a

straightforward story.

"I was on the door. It's not the main entrance, just one we use when we want to avoid a patron making a scene. The guy was escorted out and, on the way back in, the boys told me he'd groped one of the girls inside. He was heaps drunk and mouthing off something chronic. I kinda expected he'd try get back in, but no way would I let him. I was trying to let him tire himself out, then maybe order him a cab. When he kicked me, it caught me by surprise, you know? It was a strong kick, and I didn't even realise I'd hit him 'til I saw him on the ground." Nikau spoke in a high-pitched voice, totally at odds with his size. Brad didn't doubt the sincerity of his words.

"What was your intent when hitting him?" The answer to this would be crucial. Brad had the guilty act, but was there a guilty mind behind it?

"I dunno, bro, it was a reflex. Like I said, I was barely aware I'd done it. I didn't even feel an impact."

That statement meant Brad would have to see the body. Nikau averted his eyes, but Brad still caught a glimpse of tears forming.

"Can I apologise to his family? I'd want to hear it, even if it was an accident, from someone who did that to my koroua." Brad recognised the Maori word for grandfather. Brad's heart went out to Nikau. He seemed lost. Brad had never wanted to give a suspect a hug as much as he did Nikau. He seemed so respectful. Brad waited until he could regain eye contact and then told him, "I'll do what I can. I'll help you make this right. For now, you're not in trouble.

Once we've established the cause of death, we'll have another chat. But for now, you're okay. Focus on that."

Nikau nodded and wiped his face.

~

Brad looked at Jacob's face. He couldn't see any signs of significant trauma. If the punch had knocked him hard enough to kill there should be some sign of impact, surely? Jacob hadn't hit his head in the fall; he simply crumpled to the ground. That was interesting. A heavy blow should have caused him to fall to the side or backwards. Brad called the medical examiner. Unfortunately, it went through to voicemail. "Hi, it's Sam. I'm probably doing something you don't want to know about, so leave a message." Oops. Brad had unthinkingly called her personal number rather than her work one.

"Sam, it's Brad. I'll call your work phone too, but I'm at RPH with the body of a one-punch victim, or at least that's what it looks like on the security footage. I'm actually hoping there's an alternative explanation. I'll need an autopsy for an exact cause of death. I've got a copy of the footage I'll send to you."

Brad left a similar message on Samantha's work phone. It was only then he remembered he was doing the nightshift and she was probably asleep.

~

The next morning, when his phone rang, Brad leapt to answer it. He hoped it was Samantha with some fresh details for him, even though he was off duty until that evening. Instead, Dr Engels' resonant voice greeted him.

"Brad, do you remember our deal about His Majesty's Gala?"

"Don't tell me you and Sven broke up," Brad said, quickly switching his expectations from work to social.

"I'm afraid so."

"I'm sorry to hear that. Why?"

"As I told him, I didn't find myself thinking about him disproportionately to the amount of time we'd spent together."

"That really gets right to the heart of it, doesn't it? When you bring it back to that, it's not any little thing or particular issue. It's just not—"

"That's right; it wasn't love."

"I'm still sorry."

"It wasn't your fault."

"But I encouraged you to give him a go."

"And I'm appreciative of that. We had a good run, and he did help me expand my social set, which I'm grateful for."

"But now…"

Dr Engels laughed. "But now, I have no date for the gala and you're my backup."

"Hang on. I'd better get Amy in on this, so you can explain why I need to go to a ball with you while she's thirty-eight and-a-bit weeks pregnant."

Brad called his wife over and put the phone on speaker. As she struggled over Brad felt guilty for not taking the phone to her, but then he was distracted by the thought of having to wear a tux. He always felt so awkward and out of place in such garb. Growing up in the country, there just wasn't the call for such things, and his family and friends only wore suits to weddings and funerals.

"It's on Sunday evening."

"She'll be right on thirty-nine weeks then."

"What are you two conspiring about?" Amy asked.

"The Doc wants to take me on a date."

"Not just any date. To His Majesty's Theatre Gala," Dr Engels chimed in.

"You know I could pop at any moment."

"Yes, and while I have no practical knowledge of such things, I am a PhD in biotechnology, with emphasis in this case on the bio, so am at least aware that such a process takes a while, certainly enough time for a call to be placed and Brad to join you at the hospital. At the gala, we'll be within fifteen minutes of your apartment, and the hospital is only ten minutes away. You're going to Hollywood?"

"No, St John's, but it's as far away."

"So, Brad could be with you at the hospital within half an hour. That's only one or two contractions without him."

"They get closer," Amy said.

"Not at first. It builds."

"Sometimes they're quick from the start."

"Not usually for first timers," Dr Engels replied.

Amy laughed. "I can't believe I'm arguing with a gay man over *my* pregnancy!"

"Fair point. Will you let Brad keep me company? For what it's worth he'll need to frock up."

"Huh," Brad said.

"No penguin suits here. It's a fancy-dress ball, like the MET Gala. Didn't I tell you that?"

"No," Brad said with consternation.

"You'll need to wear something outrageous. Don't worry. I'm sending Julio over to kit you out. Are you home today?"

"Yes, until twelve-thirty. What have I gotten myself into?"

~

Brad had just started his shift when his phone rang again. It was Samantha.

"Steve's just emailed the findings to you, but I know you're anxious about this, so I thought I'd call too, as I countersigned the report."

"Thanks."

"The autopsy revealed massive intoxication. His BAC was 0.43, over eight times the legal driving limit. I thought the casino was going to be in trouble for that, as they should have cut him off, then I remembered he had a hip flask. Steve checked it and the tiny bit left was a grain alcohol of 70% ABV. If it was full when he started, the casino wouldn't be responsible. A check of their internal security footage should clear them. The punch barely left a mark. We think his brain was so swimming in alcohol that it was looking for an excuse to shut down. The punch was like giving it permission."

"So, did it kill him?"

"If he'd made it into a taxi, we think the same thing would have happened the moment he stopped moving. So, as the report says, intoxication was the cause of death."

"That's good. I'm sure everyone will be relieved. I know I am. The bouncer wants to speak to the family to apologise, but if he wasn't the cause, I'm not sure what to say to that."

"If he goes to them and says he's culpable, then he could give them ammunition to contest the autopsy."

"I'll ask him to write a letter, which I can vet before giving to them."

"Good idea. Before I go, have fun on Sunday."

"How do you know about that?"

"Amy sent me a photo of you being kitted out today. Seeing you standing on your coffee table being measured was so absurd it made me laugh."

"Just don't send it to my sister. She'll never let me live it down. Not only will I be in a suit, it'll be American prisoner orange with jet black lapels and cuffs."

Samantha sniggered. "That's awesome. Oh, and pics or it didn't happen."

"Don't worry. Even if her water broke, I'm sure Amy would find a way to get them."

~

Brad called his colleague, Detective Sally Summers, to his office. She sat opposite and looked at Brad with an expectant smile. Brad groaned.

"Don't tell me Amy sent them to you too?"

"Huh?"

"Nothing, never mind. Why the grin?"

"I thought you were going to say Amy's gone into

labour and you need to handover to me."

"Ah. No. Not yet. Just Braxton Hicks so far. But I do need to fill you in on the one-punch case from last night. Once I've reviewed the footage of Jacob's actions on the floor of the casino, it should be wrapped up."

"Are you nervous?"

"About the ball?"

"No, about becoming a dad. What ball?"

"Nothing. Pretend I didn't mention it. Being a dad will be a shift, that's for sure. I'm not sure how the early years will go, but I'm looking forward to answering questions when she can talk. You know, being that father figure."

"It's a girl?"

"Yeah." Brad smiled. He'd been keeping that quiet from his colleagues.

"She'll wrap you round her finger so fast."

Brad laughed. "If she's anything like her mother there's no doubt about that. But on a more serious note, is there anything else you need before taking over while I'm on leave?"

"No, just make sure all your paperwork is done. The last thing either of us want is for me to be calling you about that when you'll have far more important things to be dealing with."

Brad looked Sally in the eye. "Do you think I'll be a good father?"

Sally looked him up and down. "You are nervous aren't you? You'll be fine. Just remember. Don't try to give them everything you never had. Instead teach them what you wish you'd known."

"That sounds like something *I'd* say!"

"Yeah, well your way of looking at things is rubbing off on me."

~

Brad's next task was to review the casino's footage. As expected, it showed Jacob taking swigs from his flask. It was just an unfortunate story, and there was no legal culpability for the casino or Nikau. Brad called Nikau to give him the good news. He heard the tension in Nikau's voice when he realised who was calling.

"I'm not going to keep you in suspense. The autopsy showed the cause of death as alcohol intoxication. You didn't kill Jacob. You're free to resume your life," Brad said.

"Oh my god, thank you. Thank you," Nikau repeated.

Nikau's demeanour was so sincere Brad had the sensation, once again, of wanting to give him a hug.

He explained how the security footage cleared the casino and Nikau from responsibility. "If you still want to contact the family, you should perhaps do it via a letter. I can vet it for you, so as to avoid the risk of an inadvertent reopening of the case by Jacob's family."

"Thank you," Nikau said repeatedly at the end of the call.

~

That Sunday, Amy took dozens of photos of Brad before she let him leave. He made sure both their phones were charged and with their most shrill ringtones activated.

"You'll call me right away, right?" Brad said.

Amy grinned. "Nah, I'll be too busy cursing you for putting me in this state."

"Don't joke. I can't bear the thought of you going through it alone. I want to be there to help you feel safe … and so I can stop myself from worrying about how dangerous childbirth is for you."

Amy cupped Brad's face in her hands and looked him in the eyes.

"Our obstetrician is on stand-by. We're fine. Sure, it'll be scary, but I know you'll find a way to get there in time. Besides, as a first kid it's meant to take ages. Go have fun. You won't get another chance for a while."

~

Brad wished he had a long trench overcoat to hide his suit. He'd never felt so conspicuous as when he caught the elevator to the ground floor. The limo Dr Engels was waiting for him in appeared to be parked unnecessarily far away from the apartment. Brad got into the limo where Dr Engels was dressed in a similar suit, albeit in a slightly darker shade. His black cuffs were embroidered with red roses. He noticed Brad looking at the flowers. "My little protest to the tulip. A rose is a far superior flower anyway. Would you like a champagne?"

"No thanks. I'll have one when we get there. I want to remain sober in case I'm needed tonight."

"Given the possibilities of the evening for Amy, I must repay her for letting you out tonight."

"I think seeing me in this is enough. She's threatened

to put a framed picture of it over the baby's cot."

"You two have a good sense of humour together. My understanding is that what happens next will test that somewhat."

Brad nodded.

Dr Engels' tone shifted. "You can ask me for help if you need it." It was clear to Brad he was talking about money.

"I don't want our relationship to be like that. But, thank you, you're always very generous."

Dr Engels paused, then seeming to accept the statement, clapped his hands together and said, "So let's enjoy this last night of freedom."

"What happens at these things anyway?"

"Alcohol mostly. There will be a few speeches about the history of the theatre and why it needs support, specifically in the form of donations from everyone present."

Dr Engels handed Brad a cheque. "Here's a cheque for a thousand dollars for you to give. I have one the same. No, don't protest. This is my date, my rules. The Hartog Tulip will be unveiled, probably with a speech by you-know-who. Everyone will ooh and aah, and there will be more alcohol. Paparazzi will take a bunch of photos for the society pages, an opera company will sing a couple of songs and that will be about it."

"Okay."

~

His Majesty's Theatre was a classic example of baroque

architecture. Brad stood for a moment on the curb out the front to admire the design and the way columns were used to frame windows and balconies. He was surprised there was a thick red carpet to welcome guests. A security guard held the door open. As Brad approached, the door started swinging closed. The guard had let go of the door to greet Brad with a bear hug. When Brad was finally released, he looked up and saw Nikau, who was grinning.

"Thanks, bro," Nikau said.

Dr Engels burst out laughing. "And I thought I was the one who knew people."

"I was hoping to be inconspicuous tonight," Brad complained with mock offence.

"I couldn't miss you in that," Nikau said joyfully. "Come in, come in. If you need anything tonight, you come see me, okay?"

Brad nodded and patted Nikau on the back as he moved past him into the lavish foyer.

~

The theatre had been polished to the point of revealing the layers of its history. Brad was awed as he looked at the guests. There were at least two members of the national cricket team, several footballers, some actors and actresses and a few politicians. And then there was Athol Fugate. As tumescent and self-important as ever, he was dressed in a black suit, but in keeping with the theme of the evening was wearing a fluorescent orange tie. His fedora had a matching band around it. To Brad's eye it was somehow more naff than his own get up.

"So how do you know the security guard?" Dr Engels asked.

"Long story. Short version, he was a suspect, but we were able to prove he hadn't done it. He was grateful we let justice be served."

"Sounds familiar," Dr Engels said with a grin.

Brad laughed. "Once again, I'm sorry about that."

A waiter appeared and offered them a drink. The choice was between champagne with a slice of orange or a cola-based cocktail with the same garnish. Brad took a champagne, while Dr Engels chose the cocktail.

"This isn't a cheap champagne," Brad said.

"I'm impressed you can tell. I think it's Driscol et Dubord." Brad knew even the brands cheapest bottles cost nearly a hundred each.

"The carbonation is different, but it's also the crispness and clean taste."

"Exactly."

Brad checked his phone to make sure he hadn't missed any calls. He hadn't.

Soon enough it was time for the first speech.

~

The Lord Mayor of Perth was a sixty-year-old woman with dyed blonde hair and an ever-present grin. She bounded to the waiting lectern after the audience's attention had been drawn by a loud gong.

"Welcome one and all. There is a wonderful history to this building. It was built after a local politician, Thomas Molloy, applied to the Perth Licensing Court for planning permission to construct the theatre. Here's the thing, when he finally received permission, he promised completion within a year. This was seen as a bold timeframe, but as we know, sometimes politicians like to promise big, even if they under deliver."

There was polite laughter among the crowd.

"The winning tender was by Friederich Wilhelm Gustav Liebe, an immigrant from Saxony who had previously constructed the Bulgarian Houses of Parliament and worked on the Budapest Opera House. The tender price was £46,000, of which £43,000 was the cost of the building. Amazingly, the building *was* completed on time. Imagine that, a politician keeping their promise about the timeframe for a project!"

This time the laughter was louder.

"The theatre was officially opened at 8.00 pm on Christmas Eve in 1904 by Sylvia Forrest in the presence of her uncle, the former Premier John Forrest. Opening night saw Pollard's Opera Company perform *The Forty Thieves*, and we'll hear the Perth Opera Company sing a song from that production later. At the time of its opening, His Majesty's Theatre was the largest theatre in Australia, and was the first reinforced concrete building in Perth and, possibly the country. That's not what makes it interesting to me. What does is the rather unique cooling features installed. There were four small waterfalls located on either side of the arch, intended to cool the audience in tandem with electric fans and a retractable dome in the ceiling. Yes, the roof really did open back in the day! The dome was split down the middle, with each half sliding to either side. The artificial waterfalls were removed early in the life of the theatre, and the sliding roof was sealed when the Coalition Government undertook a $10.5 million refurbishment in 1977. The theatre was closed and reopened on 28 May 1980, with a reduced seating capacity of 1250."

The Lord Mayor paused and looked round her audience.

"Two years ago, engineers completed a detailed survey of His Majesty's Theatre and, despite the previous renovations over the years, more work was found as needing to be done to keep this magnificent theatre operational. We've been raising funds for six months now, but are still short of our goal. So, ladies and gentlemen, please open your wallets, dig deep and donate what you can to make this a reality."

Several ushers started moving from person to person. Each held a velvet bag attached to a wooden frame. They held it in front of each person until they donated. Brad watched carefully, and noted they never went to the same person twice. He concluded they must have a pre-determined zone in which to operate.

Brad dutifully placed his cheque into the bag when it was proffered to him.

Almost the moment the ushers had been to everyone, the gong sounded again, which generated an immediate hush, then a booming voice asked everyone to move from the dress circle foyer to the auditorium.

As Dr Engels and Brad made their way to edge of the tiered seating, Athol appeared centre stage, waiting to address the small crowd.

"Welcome friends, Romans, countrymen," Athol said.

Brad grimaced. Not only wasn't he a friend, the salutation just seemed crass from Athol's lips.

"It is my great pleasure to unveil the Hartog Tulip, the finest diamond anywhere in the world. When it was found at my salt mine, I was floored. It was presented as a curiosity, and it was only when we had it analysed that we realised it was actually a diamond. Finding such a gem is a highlight of my mining career, and I am thrilled to show it to you this evening. Before I do…"

Brad groaned, why couldn't he just get on with it? His mind wandered to his previous encounters with Athol and he felt himself scowl. The next words he registered were "…has now been cut to an 8.01 carat Asscher stone. I'd like to announce that I will be selling the stone and donating the proceeds to the restoration fund of this fine theatre."

Brad couldn't help but join in the applause which followed. He nudged Dr Engels. "What's his game? He'd never give up so many million without a return."

"I agree. Something's going on."

Athol waited for the applause to die down. As it started to he bowed, making it surge back up. Brad shook his head. "I can't believe people are buying this."

"Thank you. Thank you," Athol said at last. "I'd like to introduce the world-famous, Dutch supermodel, Fenna

De Jong, who is wearing the Hartog Tulip as the fastener for a cloak. Here she is."

A stunningly beautiful woman strode onto the stage. Her tanned skin, symmetrical face and long blonde hair would normally have been what caught someone's eye. Now though, it was the fact she was wearing only a white bra and panties. Across her shoulders was what looked like a white fleece, which went down only as far as her shoulders. It was mostly open at the front and clasped by a brilliant orange broach. Even from the distance of the balcony to the stage, the diamond appeared to shimmer in the light. Applause followed Fenna's entrance and continued as she stood centre stage.

"Do you think he's backlit it?" Dr Engels asked in a whisper.

"Now that wouldn't surprise me," Brad replied. "Why is he getting someone so undressed to present it? Is it so it's not scrutinised as much? Or just his idea of style?"

"Probably both."

Athol, beaming, stepped in front of Fenna. "Thank you, all. Please return to the dress circle foyer for more drinks. No wait, we have a song first."

After the opera performance, Dr Engels and Brad made their way out with the crowd, still discussing what Athol could be up to. Brad shared Dr Engels' view that somehow there was a scam of sorts going on. They just couldn't piece it together.

Dr Engels introduced Brad to a few people. Brad's regular checking of his phone was always explained with the truth that his wife was due to give birth any day now. It was amusing that most people took it as a joke and nothing more than a gentle rebuke of the older man to his younger partner. Brad ran with it. A sudden, loud scream interrupted the talking. Brad couldn't work out where it originated. A minute later, Fenna ran into the foyer from the marble stairwell leading to the entrance downstairs. She was now wearing a t-shirt and leggings, but the cloak was nowhere in sight. Brad switched to police mode.

"Where is he?" Fenna shouted. Brad paced his way over to her, with Dr Engels following. Once the crowd saw someone taking responsibility, they rapidly went back to socialising, though there were several furtive glances over to see what was happening.

"Where's who?" Brad asked.

"The man in black."

"Johnny Cash?" Dr Engels questioned incredulously.

"Who?" Fenna replied. "The man who was in my dressing room. I only caught a glimpse of him."

Brad and Dr Engels exchanged glances. "Let me guess. He took the cloak?"

Fenna looked surprised, then nodded.

Brad turned to Dr Engels. "So much for a last night off. Okay, Fenna, how about you talk us through what happened. Actually, better yet, take us to your dressing room. I'm a police officer."

Fenna led them through a maze of corridors to her room. It was a rectangular space with a chair, small table, and a large mirror, which was lit all around by LED lights.

The dimensions of the space were smaller than Brad had envisioned.

"I was getting changed into these clothes. I'd taken off the cloak and put it on the table. I was putting on my t-shirt when I saw a reflection of someone turning in the doorway. I hadn't even noticed them come in. I startled and cried out, but thought they'd come in by accident, seen me changing, and not wanting to make a scene left hoping I wouldn't notice."

Brad found himself liking her Dutch accent. The slight rolling of her 'Rs' and guttural tone were a refreshing change from the Australian drawl.

"I finished getting dressed, and that was when I noticed the cloak was missing."

Fenna didn't seem too perturbed by the incident. Brad began a slow, deliberate look around the room. Like most theatres Brad had been in, the stage and backstage area were painted black, including the walls of the room. The white cloak would have stood out on the table. But that posed a problem; if someone had taken it and been seen in the mirror, surely the cloak would be noticed too? It would contrast to the dark so much that Fenna would have noticed, unless it had been tucked into something equally dark, but from Fenna's story, there wasn't time for the person to come into the room, pick up the cloak, stuff it in a bag or under a jacket or shirt and then leave. It didn't add up.

"Can you tell me about the cloak?" Brad asked.

"It was warm for at least the areas it covered, which was

nice. There was something wrong with the diamond though; it just didn't feel like a gem." Fenna nodded sagely. "I'm into crystals but not that fake stuff like homeopathy…"

In the mirror, Brad caught a glimpse of Dr Engels rolling his eyes.

"… and it just didn't feel right. I guessed they'd made a fake version for the show. It's not unusual for us models to wear a copy of the real stones for such events."

That explained why she wasn't too worried about the theft. She thought the real stone was safe.

"I remember looking at the stone and thinking it would be good in a crown for Princess Catharina-Amalia when she becomes our queen. I put it on the table when I came into the room. Athol came to see me. I spoke to Athol for a bit. He was quite, uhh, flirty, but no that's not right, he was a bit *slordig*."

"Do you mean sleazy?" Dr Engels asked.

"Yes, that's it."

"I'm used to it. In this job it's sadly not uncommon. I told him that just because he paid me to model, he wasn't purchasing any other rights to me."

"And he left it at that?" Brad asked.

"No, but I threatened to break his penis if he tried anything. He gave up after that."

Brad stifled a laugh and appreciated the Dutchwoman's sense of forthrightness. "And the cloak was still there after your conversation?"

"Yes. No. I was a bit shaken by the confrontation, so I

didn't notice. It was a minute or so after I began changing. That was when I thought I saw someone. I thought it was Athol coming back for a second attempt, which is why I screamed, but whoever it was disappeared."

Brad smiled. "How long are you in the country for?"

"I leave on Thursday. I'm meeting with a swimwear designer for a photoshoot on Tuesday and attending the premiere of a movie on Wednesday."

"Thank you. Write your contact details on this card. I'll call you before then if I have any further questions."

~

The next morning, the papers were filled with reports about the event. There were best and worst dressed lists (Brad saw himself in the fringe of one of the photos), notes on who had attended, commentary on Athol's donation of the sale price of the Hartog Tulip and, of course, its subsequent theft.

Brad wound up having to take charge of the case, since he was first on the scene. It hadn't mattered that he'd tried to handover to a colleague, nor that he was about to start a period of leave.

Scouring the papers for details he wasn't already aware of made Brad begin to wonder if Fenna's scream was misleading him about when the stone was stolen. It was too convenient as a timestamp for the alleged theft. But Fenna had been clear she thought that was when it went missing.

There was a quote from Athol in one article saying that the stone was insured, but he wasn't sure if the conditions for a payout had been met. He promised to still donate a similar amount to the expected sale price. That had made Brad frown. He would have bet much of his savings that Athol knew he was going to get the insurance payout.

Later that morning Brad was surprised to receive a text from an unknown number. It read: Hello Sergeant. I saved your number when you called. I need to talk to you about last night. -N.

It could only be from Nikau. Brad called the number back, but it went to voicemail. A moment later he received a text: Tomorrow? 10.00 am at the address on your card?

Brad agreed, then spent the next few minutes wondering what Nikau wanted to say. At least there was the potential for a lead. At the moment there was no indication from any of the footage or reports from those in attendance to give any indication of what had happened. It was as though the cloak and diamond had vanished into thin air.

~

The next day, the papers reported that Athol would receive a multimillion-dollar payout for the theft of the Hartog Tulip, which made Brad angry. He felt himself still seething even after Amy had joined him for breakfast. Her stomach was so large, she had to sit with her chair far enough away from the table she couldn't rest her elbows on it.

"I had another Braxton Hicks contraction this morning," Amy said.

"Uh huh," Brad replied.

"I was nervous it might be the real thing, but I'm now

prepared to say it isn't."

"Yes."

"I think I might just book a caesar and get it over with."

"Yep … wait. What?"

"Have you been listening at all?"

Brad felt his cheeks flush a little. "No. Sorry."

"You look angry. Is that with me? Becoming a father? Some other reason?"

"This case with the diamond. Definitely, and only the case. You know how much I hate Athol, and it seems like he's not only going to get away with this fraud, but actually be feted for it. That makes my blood boil." He forced his face to clear, took Amy's hand and looked into her eyes. "I can't wait to be a parent with you."

Amy smiled, then burst into tears. "Hormones," she said. "I'm really happy."

~

Nikau fulfilled his commitment from his text and arrived at the station, punctually, at ten. Somehow Nikau seemed larger than Brad remembered. They sat in the interview room, even though the meeting was informal.

"Sarge, you did me a solid, so I'm gonna do you one too." He handed a backpack to Brad.

"I was on the door, as you know, and about ten minutes before the alarm was raised, I held the door for that Fugate guy. I was curious why he was leaving since it was kinda his bash. Anyway, he went round the corner where I couldn't see him. He reappeared a few minutes later, but without the bag he'd been carrying.

Brad opened the backpack. Inside was a black plastic bag. "Is this what I think it is?"

Nikau grinned in his friendly way. "Yup. I guessed he'd been to Downstairs at the Maj, you know, the theatrette which is where the name suggests."

Brad nodded. "I hunted around and found that bag under the stage."

Brad was careful not to touch the bag any more than necessary. He started using a pen from his pocket to open it further.

"Why didn't you drop it off yesterday?"

"You gave me the benefit of the doubt when it came to Jacob, and that was the right thing to do. I thought I'd give him the same, but then the paper said he was declaring it stolen and going to claim insurance."

"Thank you. Can I get you to make a statement against him saying what you saw?"

"Sure thing, bro."

Half an hour later Brad had the document signed and notarised. He took a set of Nikau's fingerprints for the next step. Brad thanked Nikau and walked him out. He then went straight to the forensics lab and handed them the backpack.

An hour later he had the evidence he wanted. Athol's fingerprints were on file due to an investigation from years before. The plastic bag contained only two sets of prints on its shiny surface: Athol's and Nikau's. With a witness placing Athol at the scene where the cloak was taken, another spotting him taking it to a hiding place, with fingerprint corroboration, the case was good. It was likely he'd be able to find a camera showing Athol carrying the bag too, if not from inside the party, then from those outside the building.

For the final piece of the puzzle Brad asked forensics to examine the stone and get a jeweller to rate it. When the result came back to say the stone was lead crystal glass, Brad knew he could charge Athol. He tried to contain his glee as he and his colleague, Detective Sally Summers, set off to make the arrest. Brad had phoned Athol and informed him he'd like to give him an in person update on the case. Athol was at a nearby hotel. He agreed to meet Brad in the foyer in fifteen minutes.

Brad and Sally were walking up the steps to the foyer when Brad's phone rang.

"Execute plan baby drop," Amy said gleefully.

"Are you sure?" Brad said.

Sally's ears must have pricked up, because she grinned at Brad and gave him the thumbs up sign, which he returned.

"Yes. These are real contractions. They hurt and are twenty minutes apart. Plus, I'm leaking."

"Can I meet you at the hospital?" Brad realised he needed to offer more of an explanation. "I'm about to arrest Athol Fugate."

"You know I'll use this against you."

"Yes. I'll be there in half an hour. I'll make the arrest but get Sally to do the formalities."

Sally, who appeared to be listening in, nodded

enthusiastically.

~

Athol was sitting in an armchair in the hotel's lobby. He didn't rise to shake their hands, instead just grunted, "Where's it at? Have you found my diamond?" Athol's smugness irritated Brad, as it always did. It seemed extra galling given he must know the gem wasn't where he had hidden it.

Brad relished what he was about to say. "Yes, Sir, I have."

The colour drained from Athol's face. "And I'm placing you under arrest for fraud."

Brad took out his handcuffs and cuffed Athol's wrists. It was a glorious moment. Athol's indignant expression and the public nature of the arrest made Brad want to fist pump the air in celebration. Instead, he helped Sally escort Athol to the police car and drove with them back to the station. After making sure they both made it into the building, he turned the car around and headed to Amy.

~

Brad couldn't stop grinning as he drove to the hospital. He'd finally pinged Athol for one of his many misdeeds. Even though Brad knew he'd fight the charge, slamming the handcuffs on Athol was immensely satisfying. Now Amy was in labour. He was going to be a dad! This was an extraordinary day. He couldn't wait to share it all with Amy.

~

At the hospital Brad was led quickly to the delivery room,

or suite as the private hospital insisted on calling it. Brad was surprised Amy was walking around the room when he arrived. Her expression changed from one of concentration to a smile when she saw him. They walked to each other and hugged.

"This is it. It's happening," Amy said.

"I know. How are you? How far along are you?"

"I'm okay. They've got me all set up for an epidural which I'm due to get sooOOON." Amy's face contorted and she gasped as a new contraction hit her. She pulled down on Brad with all her might. It took all his strength to stay upright.

A few moments later she released her grip.

"Another one down. That hurt."

Brad winced. He hated seeing her in pain.

"How far apart?"

"Twenty minutes, I think. I've had my show and waters break, so … why are you grinning?"

Brad realised his thoughts had returned to arresting Athol.

"I just arrested Athol for fraud." His grin widened at saying it aloud.

"What event are you going to be more excited by today? That or our child being born?"

Brad hesitated for a split second. Even before Amy poked him in the ribs, he knew that was a mistake. She wouldn't let him forget it either.

The Billionaires Club

A welcome silence was broken by the shrill ring of Brad's phone. He raced to pick it up. As he accepted the call, he glanced at his wife, Amy, who was breastfeeding their newborn daughter, Sophie. 'Sorry,' he mouthed. He'd worried the call would startle their daughter.

"It's okay. She's milk-drunk," Amy replied. "I'll put her down in a moment."

Brad nodded. "Greetings, Doc," he said into the phone. Brad was pleased to hear from his mentor and friend.

"Greetings indeed, Brad. How's fatherhood?" Dr Engels jovial voice replied.

Brad looked at his wife and child and smiled. "I must admit, it's been easier for me than I thought. Amy's doing the heavy lifting on the parenthood front."

Amy nodded in what Brad thought was an approving manner at his comment and waved him over. "He's actually done quite a bit," she half-whispered into the phone. Brad returned the phone to his ear.

"I may not have had the experience, but from what I understand your role is to support Amy so she can support your daughter. It seems like you're doing a good job." Dr Engels said.

"I was, but I'm back at work and we've had a few demanding cases in the last couple of weeks, so I'm not getting to everything like I did 'til now."

Brad looked at Amy who shrugged as if she'd guessed the question Brad was responding to and it was okay.

"You remember our little group, the White Tales, which met a few months ago to solve a mystery? Well, I know our next meeting was going to be in a fortnight, but my dear friend, Kersta Shi, has had an emergency and would like the help of our group *tonight*."

"What's happened?"

"She wouldn't give me all the details over the phone, but there's been a theft, which needs to be solved immediately."

"But investigations can take weeks or months. Surely she should call my colleagues."

"It's a locked room mystery, and if it got out, the scandal would ruin her. An object was stored at her place of business this morning and discovered missing three hours later. No one entered the premises between, and there was a staff member onsite the whole time."

"Oooh. Sounds intriguing. Though surely that means it's the staff member."

"They've been searched, voluntarily I might add, and nothing was found."

"What's the premises?"

"Kersta runs a club modelled on gentlemen's clubs of the past, such as the Melbourne Club. Unlike those outdated places, hers allows anyone to join. Well, anyone who is a billionaire that is."

"So how do you know about it? Are you a member?" Brad was thrilled he might finally get a straight answer to the question of the doctor's wealth.

Dr Engels sighed. "Intermittently. Membership lasts for a year at a time. Each year you need to prove you're still eligible. That's why I've lapsed before; my share price dropped around renewal time."

"And now?"

"With these unprecedented times, Kersta has forgone the requirement to existing members for this year. Which means the hundred or so members can remain if they kept their million dollar annual fee all paid up."

Brad's reply caught in his throat. "*How much?*"

Amy carried Sophie to the nursery, walking slowly so as to not disturb her.

"Yes, yes. I know it is a lot, but you're paying for exclusivity. Even amongst the twenty-one hundred billionaires in the world, membership has been denied to a few."

"Such as?"

"Such as your bugbear, Athol Fugate."

Brad scowled. "Even hearing his name makes me angry. But at least I got him for something, even if he did only get a community order, though how his lawyer managed to wrangle that instead of jail, I'll never know. He's such an—"

"Exactly. And he has been trying to get even with Kersta since she refused him. He talks down the club at every opportunity. He celebrated her forced reduction, over the last year, of locations from twelve to eight. Thankfully, the Perth one is still open. The mining magnates spared us."

"Where is it?"

Dr Engels chuckled. "A few floors above me."

"It's in the Ivory Towers?"

"Yes. It's why I'm keen to maintain membership. It's quite convenient. At its heart, it's a very well-stocked bar, but they'll order up food from any restaurant within a kilometre. There is also a concierge service which is unlike any other. They only have four staff who rotate twelve hour shifts between being onsite, given tasks out in the real world or time-off. If you need something which can only be achieved by going somewhere then that's who gets the gig. He, she or they will go and stand with someone as an order is retrieved, a name is added to a list, a specific bottle is obtained. The most outrageous thing I heard they once did was block traffic on a freeway so a member's partner would be delayed getting home, thereby avoiding catching the member with their mistress."

"That's both amazing and utterly terrible. Why would they keep them as a member?"

"That sort of thing is tolerated, as long as the person is charming. Hence no Athol, no Donald, etcetera."

Amy returned to the living room, slumped on the couch and extended the footrest. Pulling a blanket over her, she appeared to be gearing up to fall asleep watching some TV.

"Out of curiosity I once asked a concierge about hiring an assassin, and without batting an eyelid a range were offered. To this day, I don't know if they were waiting for me to call their bluff."

"They sound like people I should talk to."

"In a way that's why I'm calling. Perhaps you should put me on speaker so Amy can hear?"

Brad turned the phone's speaker on. "Hi, Amy," Dr Engels said.

"Hi, Doc."

"Kersta was very impressed when I told her about our little group and the mystery Samantha brought to us at our first meeting. She wants to present her problem to our group tonight, assuming our discretion can be assured. She's even offered to host it in the club while it's still locked down."

"But Amy and I are on parent duty for the foreseeable future," Brad exclaimed.

"The club is very happy to provide an exceptional nanny for you at no charge. They can be there within an hour."

Amy motioned to Brad. He moved the phone closer to her.

"You go. I'll look after Sophie. Doc, can you get them to replace the nanny with a housekeeper and a masseuse?

Aja's not back for another fortnight."

"Certainly. But won't you come? What if we give you those as well? You can have a night off and some extra support during the day."

"Right now, I'm so tired I'm wondering if I have narcolepsy. Also, I feel like a human cow. My brain is so fuzzy I can't think straight. Honestly, I don't think I'll be of much use, and a night off, at home, sounds like heaven. I'll pump milk for the night and then maybe I can get a few solid hours of sleep after a massage has undone the knots in my back. That would be so nice."

"I was hoping you'd come as your HR experience may be useful. Kersta can't avoid the thought her problem may be to do with personnel. Are you sure?"

"Sorry, Doc. I just don't think I could face it. Especially since I can't drink."

"Better give in, Doc. I can see in her eyes she's already daydreaming about some hunky guy massaging her, while another cleans and cooks a meal. I don't see how a night out will beat that."

"Fine. I concede. So tonight at 6.00 pm? Meet at my place and we'll go up together."

~

Dr Engels met Brad at his home a few floors below the club. Brad told him how he couldn't stop thinking about the club.

"With so few members what's the point?" Brad asked.

"The business model is surprisingly sound. Worldwide income is roughly a hundred million a year. Roughly twenty million in rent, twenty million in wages, and a budget of up to twenty million in running costs means Kersta may one day be eligible to join the club herself. There's usually no one else present when I visit. I would guess it's the same in all the other clubs. Most of the time the concierges don't have anything to do, other than maintain networks. They get to study, write or do what amuses them and they get paid around four hundred thousand a year to do it."

Brad felt his eyebrows raise. "How do I get a job like that?"

"Aside from English, you need to be fluent in at least four other languages from a range of Mandarin, Spanish, Japanese, French, German, and Russian. You'd be expected to be able to name all members by sight, be an excellent bartender and barista, and maintain impeccable standards of presentation."

"Oh."

"Not to worry. You have other skills which are needed elsewhere. Money isn't everything."

"I know, but still—"

"Let's head up. Once I show you round, you might be surprised how tedious the job would be."

~

Brad was impressed when he exited the elevator and walked down the narrow corridor to the billionaires club, which was stylised as TbC. The matte black walls were without skirting boards or cornices. The effect was of the wall extending beyond the boundaries of the floor and ceiling, making it seem as though they were about to step into something larger than the storey they were on. Brad was compelled to stop and look at the walls. Their darkness was captivating. They didn't even seem to have a sheen, despite the hallway being well-lit.

"Intoxicating to look at isn't it?" Dr Engels asked. "That's because it's painted in Black 3.0, a very special paint, which absorbs virtually all light. Kersta was quite deliberate with that choice. There is a similar paint called Vantablack, but the artist Anish Kapoor bought the rights to it, much to the annoyance of the art world. Another artist, Stuart Semple, created this paint out of spite and released it cheaply to the world."

"Spite is, unfortunately, the cause of much of my business," Brad replied.

"To this day if you buy Black 3.0 you have to sign a disclaimer confirming you're not Anish Kapoor, nor purchasing it for him."

"That's awesome."

"Wait until you see the concierge's uniform. It's made from a similarly black material called Viperblack. Honestly, I can't think of a better way to indicate prestige. Gold is so gauche. This is so hypnotic you just want to stare at it."

"What was it Wednesday Addams said? I'll stop wearing black when they make a darker colour? I'd no idea they'd managed it."

"I have a framed A2 sheet of Black 3.0 in my bedroom. It's like staring into a black hole … or the abyss."

Brad raised his eyebrows and smiled. "And what does

the abyss say back to you?"

Dr Engels chuckled. "That's for another day."

The large room of TbC also had black walls, but the ceiling and the countertop of the concierge's desk and coffee tables in the room were stark white.

"Let me guess, White 3.0?"

"Close. White 2.0. But see how its gloss and brightness makes it pop in comparison to the black."

"Yes. It makes it seem so utterly premium that I can't think of any combination to top it. The tops seem to be floating."

"Exactly. And it's the same in all of the clubs around the world."

~

TbC was, in effect, a very exclusive bar. There were a few black armchairs. Contrary to the expected leather, they were coated in Viperblack material. The carpet was the same. Dr Engels explained how difficult it had been for Kersta to get the products manufactured. She couldn't buy the patent of such a colour, instead opting to purchase the rights for using it in such applications.

Most of the group were familiar to Brad, apart from an Asian-looking woman who appeared to be in her late forties, extremely elegant and wearing a concerned expression. Next to her was a man of similar age who could only be the unfortunate concierge. Dr Engels and Brad were the last of the group to arrive. Each person sat in their own armchair, next to which was their preferred drink. No doubt the drinks had been pre-ordered by the only one who knew them all – Dr Engels. It was he who took charge.

"Welcome all to the second meeting of the White Tales. Our guest tonight is Kersta Shi, who owns this establishment. Kersta has a problem and has requested our help. If the police were to be involved, it would be disastrous. So, I'll make some introductions and then Kersta can explain what has happened." Dr Engels pointed to each member as he introduced them. "This is Brad Thomas, a detective; Jimmy 'Mug' Punter, a consultant thief; Gwyn Yang, romance author: Dr. Samantha Westlake, medical examiner; and me: Dr. Carl Engels, entrepreneur and scientist. We are the White Tales." He bowed dramatically. "Our last member, Amy, is Brad's wife, and she's currently looking after their newborn child. The gentleman to my right is Edin Sevic, one of the concierges of TbC. Kersta is a friend of mine, and I hope we can help her out."

Dr Engels indicated the raven-haired, dark-skinned woman who was tapping her fingers on the arm of her chair.

"It's unprecedented but we've been robbed," Kersta began. She spoke with the clarity and richness only a top education could provide. Edin looked forlorn. His shoulder length black hair was tied back in a neat ponytail, which only served to highlight how blotchy his pale face was looking.

"What do you mean?" Brad asked. "I should add, I'll keep this evening off the record."

254

"Thanks. Each member is allocated a safe in each of our locations. Many use them for local currency or to house things they don't want others to see. We're more secure than a bank, mostly because very few even know we exist."

Brad observed a white mark on the side of Edin's shoe, but couldn't fathom what it was.

"You say each member has a safe. How many members are there? How would a thief know which safe to break into?" asked Mug.

"There's no centralised list. The only copy of which member corresponds to which number safe is on my laptop. This laptop." Kersta tapped a sleek looking device by her side. "The laptop has had its wi-fi disabled and has top line security. It only ever connects to the internet via a tether and it hardly ever leaves my sight."

Brad took a sip of his drink. He couldn't help but admire the glassware. It was square-based and had rectangular sides. The top curved inwards to form a circular opening. Brad looked closely at his glass of water as he set it down. A visible smudge on the side indicated the surface would be ideal for obtaining fingerprints.

"What was stolen?" Brad asked.

"I need to backtrack a bit. Here's my understanding of what happened," Kersta said. "About 11.00 am this morning, Odette Malone came here for a drink and an early lunch."

Brad gave a start. "I investigated her mother's murder after our last meeting."

"Really? Carl, you must have known this, but you didn't tell me," Kersta said to Dr Engels.

"It wasn't my story to tell. Besides, you hadn't told me whose safe was broken into. What interests me is whether there's a connection between the two events."

"If there is, I know who our first suspect should be," Brad said.

"Athol Fugate," Samantha said without hesitation.

Kersta looked uncertain. "What's he got to do with anything? I mean, I know how odious he is, but—"

"I, I mean, *we* strongly suspect he ordered the hit on Yvette. Unfortunately, we couldn't get anyone to testify against him or hard evidence to prove the order came from him. He got away. Err, don't quote me on any of that. Such a personal opinion could be taken as slander," Brad said.

"I'll keep your secret if you keep mine." Kersta's anxious face, softened briefly as she gave a wry smile. "After Odette had eaten her lunch, which came from Wildflower—"

"But they only do lunch on Fridays. Today's Wednesday. They're not even open today," Gwyn exclaimed.

"They're open for us. This why our members join. After her lunch she finished some work on her laptop, extracted a USB and locked it in her safe. She then left for a meeting with her lawyers, something to do with her cousin trying to get a piece of her inheritance. That took a couple of hours. When she returned, she went to her safe to retrieve the files."

"Hang on. Why didn't she take them with her?" Gwyn asked.

Kersta's eyes darted between each member of her audience. Dr Engels broke the silence. "I'll vouch for each of the White Tales. Our discretion is assured."

Kersta sighed. "She mentioned they contain financial information she didn't want her cousin seeing. It was a precaution should they try to access her laptop. Somehow, between the time she placed it in the safe and returned to pick it up, it was taken. No one entered or left during that time."

"How can you be sure?" Mug asked.

"Edin was here the whole time."

Edin nodded as if confirming the statement.

"Forgive my asking this, Edin, but Kersta how do you know that's true?" Brad asked.

"I get an alert if he leaves. There's a lot of trust placed in his role and no physical oversight. I need to be sure someone is here twenty-four hours a day."

"How far can Edin move?" Mug asked.

"Most of the way down the corridor which led you here. When he receives an alert that a member has swiped for this floor, he is to meet them there. He's expected to be able to greet them all by sight."

"So Edin could have passed off the USB to someone," Samantha said.

Brad studied Edin's expression. He gave no signs of being concerned by the line of questioning. If anything, he seemed quite relaxed for someone whose job was likely on the line.

"There are no other logs of people arriving or leaving between the time Odette left and returned, and she left only after I arrived. I've been here since."

"Excellent. So, it really is a locked room mystery," Brad said.

"Which means the USB must still be here," Dr Engels exclaimed with delight.

"But where? I've searched the room," Kersta said.

"Did you search Edin?" Samantha asked.

"Yes."

"Everywhere?" Samantha queried.

"I even had him undo his ponytail."

"That was good thinking, but I do mean, did you search everywhere? You'd be amazed where people hide things," Samantha said with a tone that made Brad wonder just what things she'd seen.

"I didn't search his anatomy, if that's what you're asking. Let's leave that as a last resort."

Edin shifted in his seat. He looked uncomfortable for the first time. But then Brad had also shuddered at the thought of such an inspection. Thankfully, he knew Samantha would have no qualms about such a search. Performing in excess of a thousand autopsies had robbed her of any sense of impropriety when it came to examining the internals of the human body.

"How do we know something was stolen and this isn't just a hoax?" Gwyn asked. "It would make for a great plot to embarrass the club."

Kersta's skin noticeably paled. "You don't think someone would do something like that do you? To me?"

"Doc mentioned you've excluded Athol Fugate. Such petty revenge is hardly above him," Brad said.

"True," Dr Engels confirmed. "But before we start laying blame, maybe we should show them the safe?"

Kersta rose and walked to the edge of the area. She appeared to walk through the wall before a bright light illuminated a room like a star in the sky. The room couldn't be described as secret, for it had no door and was open to the room they were in, but it was nonetheless concealed due to the Black 3.0 paint obscuring any sense of depth. Brad wondered if there were other such places he hadn't noticed.

One by one they walked round the little enclave, which curved left behind the wall of the main room. Facing back where they came from revealed a grid of twelve-by-twelve safes. Each safe was about 35 cm wide and 8 cm high. In the lower right corner of each was a fingerprint scanner.

"Are we allowed to know which safe was opened?" Samantha asked.

"Number 47. Odette was given her mother's old safe."

"Have any other safes been opened?" Samantha asked.

"We don't log such things. If they were on the computer, it would provide a means for working out who owns which safe. That information is something only I have the record for." Kersta tapped her laptop, which she was carrying with her.

The group moved to return to their respective

armchairs. "Can we see the rest of the club?" Brad asked.

Kersta nodded and began showing them round.

The tour was short, due to there being little more than a bar/galley kitchen and a storage room. Brad noticed a microwave, coffee machine and fridge/freezer. As someone who took his cooking seriously, Brad was impressed with the range of premium products stocked in the pantry. Though the range was small, as most food was ordered up to the club, the quality of what was present was evident across the jams, cereals, powdered gelatin, chocolate flakes for hot chocolates, a variety of syrups, soup pouches, olive oil, and many types of vinegar and sauces on the shelves. The fridge was full, but mostly contained things to put on the sides of dishes: cream, berries and other fruits. Cow, nut and soy milks, as well as eggs, rounded out the contents.

The only other appliances in the kitchen were a toaster, microwave and set of digital scales. Brad noted the scales were accurate to 0.1 of a gram and also had a built-in timer. They were for measuring how much coffee was coming out of the machine and in what time frame. They would be placed under the china mug the coffee was flowing into, in order to ensure the optimum extraction had occurred.

"Just checking you've looked in the toaster and all the appliances?" Brad asked.

"Yes. I made Edin stay in the seating area and searched the kitchen thoroughly. You may think I don't know what that means, but I was once a forensic cleaner. I brought the attention to detail required for that job to this one. It's why I wanted the benchtops to be this white. Any uncleanliness would stand out. Shine a torch on the floor and anything even slightly reflective stands out. It was this which drove the colour scheme. Black was the perfect way to make the surfaces pop. Everything was moved, riffled through, opened and inspected."

"Okay," Brad said. "What about the storage room?"

"At the moment, it's empty apart from a washer and dryer for the hand towels, napkins and towels from the bathroom. And yes, I've looked in those as well. I even pulled out the water catcher from the condenser dryer. There's a repair kit with superglue, needle and thread, duct tape and WD-40, but it wasn't in that either."

"What about the bathroom?" Gwyn asked.

"There is a shower – the USB is not down the drain – a sink and toilet. They've all been carefully examined. I'm not shy about searching under toilet rims either, so please accept when I say this whole place has been searched. That's why I called for you. You might be able to piece something together which I cannot."

Brad noticed Samantha nod as though acknowledging a kindred spirit.

They all returned to their armchairs.

Brad couldn't stop thinking about how hard it had been to spot the entrance to the safe room, despite there being an approximately 70 cm wide entrance to the enclave of safes. Even now, looking at it, knowing it was there, he couldn't see the spot.

Samantha caught him staring at the wall. Brad quietly

told her about Dr Engels saying it was like staring into the abyss. Samantha grinned. "Nah, it's like looking at the manifestation of my sense of humour."

Brad laughed just loud enough to get everyone to look at him. He seized the moment. "What if there was someone like all those old clips of Matrix ping-pong, where people dressed in black move people and a ball on a pole around against a black background? Couldn't someone have blended into the walls here and snuck into the area where the safes are?"

Brad noticed Dr Engels nod, seemingly approvingly, at the thought.

Kersta sighed. "I doubt it. The safe room is protected by an ultrasonic sensor, which activated the camera and light a moment ago. It was never activated. That gets logged."

"So, if we accept that's true, then we have to eliminate the impossible and accept the improbable. Edin must have taken it," Brad said.

"He's been nothing but cooperative, and a loyal employee," Kersta replied.

"Can you please not talk about me as though I'm not here?" Edin asked.

Kersta nodded. "Sorry."

"What about how, err, not Edin, got into the safe?" Mug asked.

Dr Engels raised his hand slightly. "All approaches for human authentication rely on at least one of something you know, such as a password; something you have, such as a smart card; or something you are, like a fingerprint. Biometric sensors are used here. You need a fingerprint to get into your safe. So you can see, the case is impossible."

Mug sighed, then smiled. "Brad, please shut your ears for a bit. Doc, it gives me great pleasure to tell you you're wrong. The case isn't impossible because fingerprints can be copied as a research team in Japan showed. The readers can be fooled by artificial gelatin 'fingers'. I may, or may not, have used the technique successfully in my line of work."

"How?" Brad asked.

Mug laughed. "I said shut your ears. You get a clear print—"

"Like from these glasses," Brad exclaimed, pointing to a thumb print on his own glass.

"Exactly, then you scan the print, print it and fix any smudged bits with a marker, rescan, flip the image and print it onto a sticker. Stick that onto some ballistic gelatin and you're good to go," Mug said.

"But the fingerprint scanner needs a conductive substance to scan," Kersta protested.

"Yes. He probably licked it," Mug said.

"If that's so then there might still be his saliva on the scanner," Samantha said. "And where there is saliva there are skin cells and—"

"DNA," Brad said ecstatically.

"A simple PCR would give us enough to test. I could have results for you tomorrow!" Samantha said. "If you want, I can go get my kit from my car?"

Edin seemed to sink into his chair.

"Perhaps shortly. Let's see if we can solve this our way first," Dr Engels said.

"So where would the finger be now? Something that looks like a severed finger should stand out in a search," Gwyn said.

Brad smiled. "I expect he ate it."

Samantha echoed the smile. "If that's true we can prove it" – Edin's face was growing more concerned by the moment – "blood or even a stool test could show glycine, proline and hydroxyproline – the metabolites of gelatin. When we eat gelatin our blood and colon levels of them increase. But eating too much gelatin or using the wrong kind can cause constipation or bloating. Does Edin looked bloated?"

Edin looked at his stomach as if to ask if it was betraying him.

"Let's accept that as a hypothesis of what happened. It still doesn't answer where he would have hidden the USB."

"Hmm. That I don't know," Brad said.

"I do," Mug said. Everyone stared at him in amazement.

"Where?" Kersta asked.

"You said he used Odette's fingerprint and that despite a massive expense to join, the club is hardly used. Yet Doc indicated he comes here quite regularly as he lives a few floors below. If Edin could get one fingerprint why not get two?"

"But I don't use my safe? What could he steal from

me?"

"Exactly. He would know you never go into the safe room, so he hid the USB in the one other safe he had access to, one he knew wouldn't be checked."

Edin was looking paler by the moment.

"There's a flaw in that logic though. How would he know whose safe is whose?" Kersta asked.

Mug smiled. "You think you're so clever, but to a thief there's always a way to get such information. My guess would be brute force. There's only a hundred and forty-four safes. Just try them one by one. You said it wasn't logged. And then there's the matter of your uniforms. You have Edin clad head to toe in Viperblack material. Doc, you might know more about this than me, but since it absorbs light, would it also absorb sound? As in ultrasonic sound?"

"Maybe a little more than ordinary material, but I'm not certain."

"Well, there you go. If he moved slowly as well, then not enough 'shifted' sound energy would reach the receivers on the sensor to trip an alarm. It's that simple. It's a very effective defeat technique. Actually, with enough practice he could do it without the suit. Given how much free time he gets, why wouldn't you amuse yourself and see if you could move around the room without setting it off?"

"But why would he do it? I mean he's paid a fortune," Brad said.

Gwyn smiled. "If you worked here every day, bored as batshit, then some entitled toff comes in and you have to serve them like they're the king or queen of the fucking world, why wouldn't you take a chance to earn a swift few million?"

"Why that amount?" Brad asked.

"You told me Doc had said earlier the concierges are paid between four and five hundred thousand a year. If you were going to end your career, you'd want to do it for enough to make it worthwhile. With that income I'd guess it'd be around five million."

"But we still haven't checked Doc's safe. Surely all this conjecture is worthless without evidence?" Samantha said.

"But we have evidence," Brad replied. "There's the superglue which could be used to reveal or strengthen the image of the fingerprints. All you need is an enclosed space. The microwave would suffice. Squeeze out some glue and the fumes create a powdery residue which sticks to the prints. Edin might claim it was for his shoe, which I think has a white glue mark on it, but its presence there could be cover for why the glue is in the club. There was gelatin powder in the pantry, which could make ballistics gel in the right concentration. He has a printer, scanner and computer at the front desk. There are all the resources necessary here."

"Well, let's test the theory. Doc, would you do the honours?" Kersta asked.

Brad was sure Edin's face was shinier than before. Was he sweating? As Dr Engels went into the safe room, Brad once again marvelled at how he seemed to walk through the wall. An instant later a bright light appeared, like a star in the sky. It was a strange effect. The ceiling was white, but with the light directed to the black materials there was no reflected light to illuminate the rest of the room. A few moments after that, he emerged with a face Brad could see he was struggling to keep neutral. The upturned edges of his mouth gave him away before he made the announcement.

"Is this what you were looking for?"

He held out a shiny maroon USB memory stick. It had what looked like a diamond encrusted into its flattest edge.

"That's it. That's how Odette described it," Kersta said elatedly. She turned to Edin and scowled. "Who were the plans stolen for? You wouldn't do this on a whim? Was it the cousin?"

"No," Edin said. He lowered his eyes. His gaze seemed to become absorbed by the floor.

"Then who?"

"You've mentioned him already."

Brad felt his face drop. "Athol?"

Edin nodded. "He wants the financials so he can convince Odette to sell her mother's, I mean her, uranium mine to him. She's been resistant to his advances."

Brad felt a hot wave of anger rise in him. "That's because he murdered her mother in the belief he could get Odette to sell afterwards. He wasn't expecting her to take on running the company."

"From what you've said, he's such a snake he's probably behind the cousin suing Odette. It would also explain how he might guess the information would be here," Gwyn said.

"Now that's White Tale thinking," Dr Engels said, beaming with pride. "Kersta, when you call Odette you might want to let her know he may be behind her cousin's lawsuit. My guess would be the suit gets dropped pretty quickly."

"I will," Kersta said.

Edin turned to Gwyn. "Since I'm sunk, you might be happy to know the payment was ten million."

Gwyn raised her glass and acknowledged the statement before taking a sip.

Brad's eyes lit up. "I need to get you on record about that." The pitch of his voice probably betrayed his excitement that he might be able to arrest Athol again. The last time had been so satisfying, even if Athol spent only spent one night in jail before his lawyers negotiated bail and a plea deal that saw him get away with a two-year good behaviour bond and community service.

"What about Edin?" Kersta said.

"I was going to arrest him, get him to sign a statement to say Athol put him up to it," Brad replied.

"No." Kersta was resolute. "The scandal isn't worth the prosecution. Edin will, of course, be fired. But no word of this can get out. You cannot press any charges."

Brad's mood turned dark. He knew he had the right to press charges without Odette's cooperation, but it would be nearly impossible for them to succeed without her help. The other White Tales had sworn discretion, which they were unlikely to break. He had no case, which meant Athol got away with yet another crime. Brad furrowed his brow.

"But Odette will know," Samantha said. Then seemingly reading Brad's expression added, "and Athol's scheme has been thwarted."

"Edin, is it possible to recreate Odette's fingerprint? Especially if I let you keep the money," Kersta said. Edin's eyes lit up and he nodded enthusiastically. Kersta smiled. "Then we will replace the USB into her safe and make it seem like she just missed it. Whether she believes it or not is beside the point. She will *have to* accept that as the story. I'll then say some unnamed source has warned me Athol is behind her cousin's lawsuit. Thank you, Carl and White Tales. You have saved my reputation." She turned to Edin. "You have two hours left on your shift. I suggest you start them by making us another round of drinks. It will take me a couple of months to recruit a replacement for you. Since I'm refusing prosecution, you will keep doing your job, without pay, until then."

Edin's mouth fell open. After a pause, he closed it and said, "Yes." He stood and went behind the bar.

"White Tales, your group intrigues me. As a thank you for your help tonight, please feel free to organise your future meetings here and … maybe I could sit in on them occasionally? Or be a guest? I have some good stories from my days as a forensic cleaner."

They looked at each other and nodded. It was agreed. The White Tales had found their home.

Acknowledgements

This book is almost an accident as I wasn't intending to write another short-story collection anytime soon. One day, I was daydreaming about the urban legend of a scuba diver being found dead in a tree in a forest and thought it would be cool to write a story like that. My version of that tale is told in *Blue*. After that, I kept thinking of other ideas. I'd had the article on poison fire coral saved for ages, and somehow within a couple of weeks I had ideas for most of the stories in this collection. The setting for the last story, The Billionaires Club, was based on a dream I had about such a location. I wrote the story with no idea of what I was going to write about other than the setting. Over several redrafts, I had fun turning it into a locked room mystery.

I've made reference to some of the sources of ideas in the stories themselves, some more direct than others. The stepmum in *Fuller* is an engineer who has lost her thumb. This is a subtle reference to a Sherlock Holmes story called *The Engineers Thumb*, which also references Fuller's earth, a key plot point of my story.

Cannabinoid hyperemesis made its way into the Billionaires Bath after I read about it in a book called *Every Patient Tells a Story: Medical Mysteries and the Art of Diagnosis* by Lisa Sanders. I'd been trying to think of a reason why someone would spend so much time in the bath and read about the condition at just the right time in writing the story. A case of serendipity, or *synchronicity*, if that's what you prefer.

The discussion of paints in *The Billionaires Club* is based on real events in the art world. I was so inspired from my research in that area, I bought some Black 3.0 and White 2.0 to create my own piece of art.

Working with my editor, Kathryn Moore has again been invaluable. She knows how to bring out the best in my writing and is great to work with. My proofreader/line editor Kim Smith did a great job picking up typos numerous reads had missed.

I'd also like to thank the Monash Writers Group for their encouragement and support. They read half the stories and gave great feedback on them. I'd like to thank my children for keeping me grounded and being two wonderful human beings. My gratitude goes to Marc Testart and Dr. Rebecca Omura for their legal and medical advice respectively. While I still took some creative licence, I'm grateful for their comments on my early ideas and their stopping me from going down a path that was at best implausible, or at worst, impossible. Similarly, I'd like to thank Professor Andrew Russell who helped me correct some technical mistakes I'd made when discussing

Viperblack material. And just because I stole his joke about outlaws, I'd like to give a shout out to Craig Moore. Though, while I'm at it, I should also thank the rest of the old school crew in Ken Chu and Wijiv Thuraisingham.

In the previous *Colours of Death* collection, the black and white themed stories had a different outcome compared to the others. I've repeated that here but also made those stories different in structure through the introduction of the White Tales.

All the medical conditions and effects of chemicals and poisons described in these stories are real. All science discussed is based on real studies and research, though I've applied some aspects in new ways, which may or may not hold true in real life.

I hope you've enjoyed reading this book. If you have, please leave a review on Amazon, Goodreads and social media.

About the Author

When he was in high school, a dare escalated a little too quickly and Robert made the state final in an interpretive dance competition. Thankfully, his teacher was okay with him chickening out of the main event, thus preserving his affection for education. Whilst not a direct consequence, Robert has since spent too much of his life studying and is undertaking his seventh university degree, a PhD in Education. Robert has degrees in psychology, sociology, biology and education, all of which inspire his writing.

Robert studied Wado-Ryu karate for twenty years and ran his own dojo in Perth for several years. However, he is not currently training.

Robert is kosmemophobic, meaning he has a fear of jewellery. He has no idea why; it just freaks him out.